Divine Madness

The Quantum Mechanics of the Soul

A Novel (Broadly Speaking)

Joseph G Mazzilli

Published in the United States by Joseph G Mazzilli. First paperback edition October 2025

ISBN 979-8-9932320-2-7 (e-book)

ISBN 979-8-9932320-0-3 (paperback)

ISBN 979-8-9932320-3-4 (hardcover)

Cover Image by NASA

Cover design and internal formatting by Sam Richard

CELEBRITY ENDORSEMENTS

When we remember that we are all mad, the mysteries disappear and life stands explained.

— Mark Twain

The capacity for self-reflection is given to man alone...that is why he has, so to speak, the privilege of madness.

— Friedrich Hegel

Men are so necessarily mad that not to be mad would only be another form of madness.

— Blaise Pascal

Certain attainments of the soul and the intellect are impossible without disease, without insanity, without spiritual crime.

— Thomas Mann

No Prelate's lawn with hair shirt lined is half so incoherent as my mind.

— Alexander Pope

It seems that God took away the minds of poets that they might better express his.

— Attributed to Socrates

We do not have to visit a madhouse to find disordered minds; our planet is the mental institution of the universe.

— Johann Wolfgang von Goethe

My story...has the taste of nonsense and chaos, of madness and dreams—like the lives of all men who stop deceiving themselves.

— Herman Hesse (*Demian*)

There is so much in man that is hideous! Too long, the earth has been a madhouse.

— Friedrich Nietzsche

The soul demands your folly, not your wisdom.

— Carl Jung

Acknowledgements

The author would like to thank the many friends and family members who offered kind words of encouragement throughout the writing. A special thank you to Andrea Savage and Michael Harrison, who proofread the entire novel—still a challenge to read, but especially challenging at the early stages—and suggested numerous corrections. The author bears all responsibility for anything that still needs correction. And thank you to my Princeton classmate, Amy Perlin, for her helpful comments about Judaism.

Above all the author wishes to thank his beloved wife, Kim, for her constant support and encouragement since the very beginning.

Contents

Prologue

Though this pen
Did never aim to grieve, but better men;
Howe'er the age he lives in doth endure
The vices that she breeds, above their cure.
But when the wholesome remedies are sweet,
And in their working gain and profit meet,
He hopes to find no spirit so much diseas'd,
But will with such fair correctives be pleas'd:
For here he doth not fear who can apply.
If there be any that will sit so nigh
Unto the stream, to look what it doth run,
They shall find things, they'd think or wish
     were done:
They are a madman's follies, but so shown,
As even the sane may see, and yet will own.

— Ben Jonson

MY WIFE MARY AND I COULDN'T HAVE *REAL* CHILDREN. Now, after giving birth to this book, I finally understand

1

how it must feel to have a child. If I happen to see you reading it, I'll probably wrestle it from your firm grasp and say, "Look at you. Just look at you. I'm ashamed to say I'm your father. Let me fix your collar, and let's pat that hair down (blood of my blood, we have the same horrible cowlick). Did you brush your teeth this morning? My God! Look at those dirty fingernails." I'm speaking figuratively of course (I got a little carried away; I promise it won't happen again), for the fretful way I'd grab a pen from my shirt pocket and try to make the book more presentable, deleting a word here, adding a word there, tidying up a paragraph or two, and maybe adding some footnotes.

You hold in your hands a new life form, a result of recombinant literary engineering, a breakthrough that was bound to follow genetic engineering sooner or later. But I should warn you that a breakthrough always looks like a breakdown to the uninformed (especially to the one having it). Those already familiar with recombinant literary engineering can take a short intermission to freshen up, because this is a very important concept, and I don't want to leave the other readers behind. For those who haven't heard of it, don't be alarmed. Recombinant literary engineering is just the technical term for when a work of literature, deliberately or not, doesn't make any sense.

Nietzsche said that out of profound weariness in our search for the truth, we sometimes embrace a lie. Now we have embraced the lie that life has no meaning. "All is chaos," we say. Man is in a forest called reality and can no longer see the forest for the trees. I stand outside the forest. Every possible combination and *permutation* of literature has tried to give order to the universe and meaning to our lives. But all they have done is whet our appetite.

Literature needs a *mutation*. The truth is buried so

deep in the chaos that you can't dig it up with scalpels and dental picks. You can't find it with Nietzsche's tuning fork. You need a bulldozer.

Knowledge has grown so fast and so vast
That it's reached a critical mass, like uranium.
And there's too much to organize in our cranium.
You hold in your hands the high-grade plutonium
That can rocket us out of the pandemonium.

Like Nietzsche's Superman, Zarathustra, I roam where I please to pillage literature, and like the Old Testament's Jeremiah, I root it up and destroy it to rebuild it. But to keep my editor from pulling his hair out, and so that he could save face over at the Editor's Bar & Grille, the "structure" alludes to the ancient Greek precursor of the novel, the Menippean satire, which always included some light verse.

In a nutshell--forgive my redundancy, everything I say is literally in a nutshell--you have to stand on another planet to see ours clearly. That's the main reason I think NASA might try to kidnap me for their space program. I'm already there.

Introduction

Whoever believes himself mad when he is not, is mad by virtue of that very belief.

— Shoshana Felman

You'd be there too, if God spoke to you. I should hasten to add that it was not the God of *any* religion. Indeed, what he said would be heresy in most religions. And he is most definitely not a he, a she, or an it for that matter. I was raised in the Catholic church. So even though I am no longer a Catholic, nor a Christian, I can't help but see God as an old grandfatherly figure. But that is only a mask, an avatar, that I make God wear. So please don't mistake my use of the grandfather mask for the actual God—to borrow from Judaism, the *Ein Sof*, God the Unknowable.

God didn't speak in words, of course. If I had to put it in words, I'd say it was similar to the famous cartoon by James Thurber, of a plump, middle-aged man who thought he heard a seal barking behind his headboard. Except in my case, while the man *was* middle-aged or at least *late*-middle-aged, he wasn't plump, there was no sound and it didn't come from behind the headboard.

On second thought, it wasn't that similar, but nothing else even comes close. The non-visual, non-auditory, divine communiqué came from somewhere in the kitchen (at first I thought something was wrong with the refrigerator). And to say I "wasn't plump" is a *Litotes*, a polite way of saying that the other reason NASA might try to kidnap me is for their weightless experiments, because I'm practically weightless already. In my youth and early adulthood I looked like a toothpick. This kitchen episode happened ten years ago, when I was fifty-seven. By then I had filled out and looked like a Popsicle stick. But now at sixty-seven, I've filled out even more and I look like a beanpole. Well, maybe a fava beanpole.

(Readers who share my philological ken will recognize *Litotes*, a singular noun with an "s" on the end that expresses the negation of the opposite of the intended meaning. So "not a warm day" means "a cold day." Truthfully, I'm almost positive that I do not have a philological ken; words pop into my head with no rhyme or reason.)

If the FBI commandeers your car to chase a fugitive, you don't argue. If the DEA commandeers your boat for a drug interdiction, you don't argue. And similarly, if God, with all the choices available to him, decides to commandeer a potentially certifiable crazy person to be the official tour guide to the soul, who am I to complain?

But I did complain. I said, "This isn't God; this is some sort of mental breakdown." The thought occurred to me that I probably needed a straitjacket and some very soothing music. Kierkegaard said that when God speaks to you, you should not make him sit in the waiting room, like you're some important doctor, while you decide if it's really him. For once I agree with Kierkegaard. God did not have to sit in my "waiting room" very long before I grabbed a broom from beside the refrigerator and tried to chase him out of my little bungalow.

I shouldn't have to tell you that an argument ensued. I wish I could say I won. I wish I could say, "That's right. I'm in charge now. Omniscience is one rung below madness on the evolutionary ladder." But this is not a work of fiction, in spite of what it says on the cover, so I have to tell the truth. The publisher's legal department said they had to call it a novel to comply with the truth-in-advertising laws, because they think I live in a fictional world.

Great discoveries take time to be understood. Scientists recently discovered that gypsy moths, with brains between the size of a pinhead and a matchhead, communicate over distances that sight, sound and even pheromones can't reach. There have been many other discoveries about the uncanny abilities of dolphins and household pets, and even about telepathy in rats. Combine them with the concept of *quantum entanglement* (Einstein's "spooky action at a distance") in physics and it's easy to see how these discoveries will soon throw a monkey wrench into the mind-body debate, concerning whether or not the mind is more than the sum of its parts. Then the publisher's legal department will finally understand how it's possible for God to speak to a human. And this book will no longer have to say "A Novel" on the cover.

We're moving at quite a pace here. Some of you are probably delirious by now. I know how that feels, because I was born that way. And some of you are probably confused. "Yeah, sure," you're thinking, "the quantum mechanics of the soul explained by a crazy person. Why does every book proclaim itself as the Holy Grail, the pearl of great price and the living waters that you have thirsted for all your life, only to turn around and slam you pell-mell into another brick wall?"

Jung explained it best. The writer's overactive imagination comes from watching too many cartoons in his formative years, where The Brick Wall assumes the stature of a religious icon. Children find nothing so ecstatic as watching someone slam into a brick wall, after being fooled by a trick road sign, or more commonly by a false mural of a road painted on the wall itself. The writer's refusal to get a real job is *ipso facto* proof that he is trapped in this childhood world. I'm not a hundred percent sure that Jung said it, but I'm pretty sure he would agree.

Don't worry, I'll show you the hand and footholds to climb over the wall. Confucius said, "In seeking a foothold for self, love finds a foothold for others; seeking light for itself, it enlightens others also." Those readers who aren't confused can go amuse themselves for a few minutes, while I give the others a boost.

As we begin our climb, I must ensure
The hand and footholds, so all endure.
Not every hand can hold the same brick,
Nor can every foot fit the same niche.

Mary and I were married on June 3rd in 1978, just before college graduation. For wedding presents, her friends gave her all sorts of gardening implements. She loved gardening. It's a great way to occupy time. Our wedding was at the cemetery in Cedar Mills, New Jersey, about a week after her funeral.

That was around forty-five years ago. Some classmates

staged the wedding to humor me in my grief. Before she died, we were engaged. We shared a sense of humor, especially about religious matters, and our friends thought that she, or her ghost at least, would enjoy the gravesite wedding. Our real wedding invitations, mailed shortly before the car accident, announced that Mary Ruth Malin and Joseph Colocento were to be married on June 10th, in the Unitarian Church of Princeton, "neutral territory for our Jewish and Catholic relatives," we said.

For her sixty-sixth birthday, which was last August 2nd, I took a train from my home in Saint Augustine, Florida to the cemetery where she was buried in New Jersey. I bought her a size XXXL tee shirt, so I could slip it over her gravestone. It said, "I'm Recycled." As I slipped it on, I could hear her cosmic laughter. I laughed too, I think. I have so many nostalgic reflections that it's hard to sort out the real ones. In all honesty, I have to admit that we're an unusual couple.

Hungry for answers to the meaning of life, if for no other reason than to make sense of Mary's death, I dug everywhere, like a dog--a mad dog--looking for bones, and I found a few small bones in every hole. Now I have the whole skeleton. The deepest hole I dug was in my own mind. I'm a cranial geologist, and I'm happy to report that the subsurface explorations are complete.

This brings me full circle to my central discussion (don't expect one every time) about my argument with God. It wasn't a verbal argument, but I'll try to translate it anyway. Imagine two gypsy moths having a non-verbal, non-visual, non-tactile and non-olfactory conversation (perhaps they are in a state of *quantum entanglement*). One's about six feet tall and a hundred and forty-two pounds. He doesn't fly. In fact he's afraid of flying. If he has to travel far, he takes the train. Mostly he just walks around fidgeting. That's me. Now for the hard part. Suddenly, the sky turns dark, and the entire universe as we know it is eclipsed by what can only be described as the "Holy Mother of all Moths." That's You-Know-Who.

And you thought I was mad. You should listen to him. Buddhism teaches that the perfect mind is at rest. Since thinking is a process by which we come to know, the perfect mind doesn't have to think. Where on earth did they ever get this idea? God's infinite and omniscient mind, not limited by space or time, is on everything at once. (My doctor advised me to stay away from Buddhism, because they teach detachment, and he says I'm far too detached already.)

I talk in circles. Doctor Christiane Northrop said that people who talk in circles may take longer to make their point, but when they finally do, it will be a richer experience for the listener. At least that's what I think she said. God talks in spirals. When he's feeling expansive, he works out from the center. What follows is admittedly an oversimplification, but I assure you I did not put words into his mouth. I took them out. Had I not, this book would stretch from earth all the way to the planet I seem to be from.

The Kitchen Episode

It is of great benefit to the soul, working in secret, that at the height of consciousness it moves away from consciousness.

— Friedrich Hölderlin

LITTLE MOTH (ME), WITH A NERVOUS FLIT-FLIT OF HIS *tiny wings:* "You idiot. Now you did it. I didn't drop those coffee beans this time. I saw them jump right off the refrigerator shelf and onto the floor. Explain that, will you. I've suspected you for a long time. No one can be as clumsy as I seem to be, always dropping things, getting my shoelaces tied together and my belt all tangled up in my pant loops every morning. Finally, I caught you red-handed. I can't believe all that codependent blather they say about you, 'He chastens those he loves; he's purging me with hyssop; he's purifying me in the crucible; he's the potter and I'm the clay; weeping endureth for a night, but joy cometh in the morning.' I am not one of your enablers. Now clean them up, or they'll lie on the floor till you do.

Big Moth (God): Utter silence, but I had a palpable feeling that he was sulking.

Little moth, about an hour later, feeling a little gutsy, since God didn't strike him with lightning after the first remark: "And don't even try to weasel your way out of last year's Macarena episode. The fire department had to untangle my arms and legs with a come-a-long, while the whole school stared in disbelief. It couldn't be that hard, I thought; even the blind kids were doing it. So why shouldn't a fifty-six-year-old volunteer chaperone be able to do something as simple as the Macarena?"

(Saint Augustine is home to the renowned Florida School for the Deaf & the Blind. For some years I had volunteered on occasion to tape-record books that they could not get from the Books on Tape organization. My reading for them is generally no longer needed, since anything available digitally is read for them on their own digital devices by software that was developed for that purpose, such as JAWS. But on rare occasions I am still needed. I like to read, so it has been a volunteer match made in heaven.)

Big Moth, with an ear-deafening FLUB-FLUB of his Concorde-sized wings: "Joseph, if you weren't hiding under the dining room table, you'd see I'm waving a white flag, the sign of surrender."

Little moth, puffing up his thorax, in the way David might, after striking Goliath with his slingshot: "Well, it's about time. They've been sitting there for over an hour now. You'll find the broom and the dustpan by the refrigerator."

Big Moth, rolling his compound eyes, and muttering to himself, so that you could barely see his proboscis moving (it looked like the Eiffel tower swaying ever so slightly in a strong breeze): "Not the coffee beans, Joseph; I had nothing to do with that. I meant about coming here. It's against the rules."

Little moth, with all six arms, three on each side, akimbo: "I heard that. What rules?"

Big Moth, with all six arms, the size of construction excavator arms, akimbo: "They're not my rules; they're yours. Remember when your father taught you to bat a ball? First he pitched the ball underhand, and slowly. Then he gradually built up speed, and finally pitched it overhand. And you said, 'Throw me a fastball, Daddy. I can hit it.' And when he taught you to play cards? He let you win at first, and only gradually made you play by the rules. And you said, 'Don't let me win, Daddy. I want to play by the real rules.' That's what your soul thought it was ready for in coming here."

Little moth, with his little compound eyes practically bulging out of their sockets, and his mouth spewing saliva (not due to madness, but to a misaligned jaw from the car accident), as he interrupted God: "You're a bigger idiot than I thought. Was Mary's death a game? Was the truck that my car went under your idea of a fastball, and my poor roommate, Tiger, a game? He sits around like a vegetable. I nicknamed him Tiger in college, because he was fast and stealthy like a Tiger. And he was as ferocious as one, especially when he'd spend hours beating on that crazy Wooden Dummy Kung Fu contraption that he had in our dorm room. Now he's fatter than a Panda, from sitting around like a zucchini. I talk to him as though he can talk back, hoping Goethe was right when he said to treat someone as you imagine he could be, and he'll rise to it. But now I know what's wrong. Tiger's just sitting there thinking about the accident, saying, 'Whoa, what kind of curveball was that?' That's why I yelled and screamed at you all these years. You took my Mary. And you might as well have taken Tiger. She spent most of her short life trying to make sense of your 'role' in The Holocaust. She said she saw you in a flash of lightning when she was twelve years old. I thought she was as crazy as I was, until she beat me and Tiger at pool by shooting all the balls into a central hub on the table. We thought she was some sort of magician, but she said it was from her work on the nature of God. (Her senior thesis was titled *Chaos Theory and the Nature of God*.) Was she an umpire about to bench the pitcher for six million bad throws? So you ran up to her behind home plate and bashed her brains in with the bat?"

Big Moth, with tears the size of kidney-shaped swimming pools forming along the circumference of his compound eyes: "Now Joseph, you have no idea what you're saying. I have many other universes out there, beyond this one, all in various stages of expansion and contraction. But in this one alone, there are Holocausts, and car accidents. At this very moment, in this universe, in distant galaxies, there are Holocausts occurring, each involving many souls. And they make me weep. Genocide in all its forms and degrees is one of the saddest things about this universe. Understand that when something makes me sad, I am infinitely sad. My heart bursts like a giant supernova. There are places along your soul's journey, in other universes, where I do swoop down like Superman to prevent evil, and car accidents, but not here. Everyone's fond of saying that I'm the 'unmoved mover.' What a comforting thought, but it's just the opposite. Here, I'm the moved unmover. Everything is real here and has to obey the laws of nature. It wasn't my nature that Mary stumbled upon while playing billiards. That was the Federal Express hub system. It's very efficient, but not divine. This is the last stop before your soul returns home, like a drop of water returning to the sea. There are rapids and waterfalls and all sorts of rough spots along the way, but nothing as rough as the final inlet into the ocean. The return to the womb is just as painful as the birth, for the mother as well as the child. It's not a game. It's not a 'growth opportunity,' as some of you call it. No one's 'karma' deals the hand they're given. It's random, because you want it that way. For one brief instant in your soul's very long life, longer than you have numbers to describe, you want to know what it feels like to live in a real world. Like the child begging for a fastball, or a real poker hand, you all beg me to come here. 'You treat me like a paper doll,' you cry. 'When can I live in a real world?' There are so many stages along your journey, places where there is no evil, where there are no accidents of birth, of life, or of death, on down to intermediate stages that are more and more real, until you finally come here. Heaven is not the end of your journey; it's the maternity ward. I'm the beginning and the end. But this is your last stop; I have many others like it."

Little moth, pacing wildly about the house, from the kitchen to the dining room to the living room, then into his bedroom, then into Tiger's bedroom, where Tiger sat looking out the window, even though it was dark out, then back to the kitchen, pacing for what seemed like hours, but it all took place in nanoseconds, as he slowly, with his syncerebral brain, absorbed Big Moth's words: "The Federal Express hub system? And all this time I thought I was mad, because it made no sense to believe in you. But I did believe, not in my head, but in my gut. I stopped believing in you in high school. But my Catholic upbringing remained in my gut like a cancer in remission. Mary brought it out of remission, partly with her almost magical command of the pool table. But still, my head and my gut were at war. In college I idolized Professor Kaufmann, who idolized Nietzsche, who said you were dead. I didn't think you were dead. It made better sense to think you never existed. And yet I yelled and screamed at you every time I saw a redhead on the street who reminded me of Mary, and every time I thought I heard Tiger say something, when it was only the wind, even though intellectually, I knew that you didn't exist. 'It's schizophrenia, of course, that's it,' I'd tell myself, 'I have to be crazy.' But I'm not? Tell me I'm not."

Big Moth, gesturing with his wings for little moth to sit down, as though he were about to deliver some bad news: "Joseph, in the whole history of this planet, indeed of this entire universe, your years and years of constant ranting and raving at me far exceeds anyone else's. In that sense you are mad—mad as in 'angry.' And you must admit, yelling and screaming for years and years at a God in whom you don't believe sounds a little crazy as well. But if you mean 'reality challenged,' then I don't have an answer. You're a bold new experiment that nature is conducting. I know there's a fence separating the subconscious from the conscious, because I built it with my own hands. The conscious is like a corral, where thoughts parade around like tame horses. You filled your conscious mind beyond its capacity—I'm not saying that its capacity is especially large or small, and . . . I've already told you more than I should. I'm taking a calculated risk that you can keep our visit a secret, but if you can't, then everyone will think you're having another one of your episodes. That's one of my little loopholes; I can provide a little extra comfort to those who, for various reasons, will never be able to tell on me, and to those who will never be believed if they do tell."

Little moth, with tiny feet fidgeting wildly, as though he had just set all six of them at once on a hot light bulb:

"What? You mean I'm really mad? I knew it. I knew it. Those idiots at Princeton said that they had some students and faculty who were so brilliant it bordered on madness, as well as some who were so mad it bordered on brilliance. But they told me that I wasn't mad. They said, 'Be assured that you're not mad.' It was Princeton, wasn't it? My everyday existence is constantly informed by so many nostalgic reflections that it's hard to believe one person could have done so much. Didn't I build the Panama Canal? I seem to remember something about that. But I'm sure I went to Princeton. I remember no one else would take me."

Big Moth, rolling on the floor laughing, and kicking all six of his feet in the air in convulsions: "Oh, of course you went there. No one else *would* take you. All the other colleges thought that you were so mad it bordered on brilliance, not the other way around. Princeton saw it too. 'His thoughts gallop around in his head like wild horses,' they said, 'but we can tame them.' Soon, they thought, they would have your horses walking in calm circles and doing tricks. But as usual, you weren't paying attention. They didn't say, 'Be assured that you're not mad.' They said, 'We're not sure that you're not mad.'"

If I might digress for just one brief moment, I should tell you that in my youth I read too much. I was by no means a fast reader. The real *Rain Man*, Kim Peek, who could read two pages at once in about ten seconds, would get no competition from me. I just read a lot. I read to make new friends. I hesitate to say *imaginary* friends, but they were at least very *literary* friends. My classmates were friendly enough, but they could never, or at least *would* never invite me into their lives and adventures in the way Tom Sawyer and Huck Finn did. While reading I hung my feet over the edge of my bed to feel the Mississippi river swish through my toes as I floated along with them on the raft. I practiced the "mind control" I learned from Hesse's *Demian* on my father, so he wouldn't catch me reading it while I was supposed to be cleaning sawdust off the tools in his basement woodshop. When Tuesday Lobsang Rampa got *The Third Eye* from the Tibetan Lamas, I imagined that I could see people's auras and levitate just like he did. I remembered a lot of snippets, but I had great trouble organizing my thoughts, and I spouted a lot of nonsense. You'd think that Princeton could tell the difference between brilliance and madness, but they really couldn't. It's not their fault; we're intersecting sets.

My father was a simple, salt of the earth carpenter, not some sort of genius. He just had common sense, but he *could* tell. He'd say, "Joseph, you're crazy, son. Come help me install Mrs. Feaster's bookcases this weekend. Working with your hands always seems to calm you down." The school counselor told him I was reading too much, after I turned in a two-page, eighth grade paper with too many footnotes. I'm not saying that it was a *good* paper; just that it had too many footnotes. In fact my entire academic career, from the earliest beginning until the very end, and I must admit, my home life during that period as well, was marked by the constant refrains, "Joseph, you didn't understand a word I said," and "Joseph, you're not making any sense." (A lie of omission. I promise it won't happen again. These refrains can still be heard today.)

My father's intelligence could not be measured by book learning. In school he went as far as sixth grade. At home he did not sit around at night reading *Popular Mechanics*, as some fathers did. He smoked a pack a day of Marlboros, and at night he watched John Wayne movies and Archie Bunker on TV. But he was a Master Carpenter, and an absolute perfectionist. After learning his trade since childhood, and practicing it for years and years, he had the sort of muscle memory that Olympic athletes have, where he could lay out and cut stair stringers and roof rafters, build custom Formica cabinets, rabbit doors for hinges, and all sorts of other carpentry skills, without thinking. He had a certain self-assuredness, common sense and wisdom that carried over from his work into all aspects of life. Tiger admonished me all through college—I can't remember if it's from the Tao or Confucius—to dig one deep well in life, and then I would hit water. Tiger did that with his Kung Fu.

He'd say, "Joey, you try everything, but you never stay with anything. You dig a hundred shallow wells and you never hit water. Why do you try to play the congas, try to be an artist, try sailing club, try gymnastics, try everything, but never stay with anything? That's an awful lot of work with nothing to show for it."

My father may have consciously emulated Archie Bunker and John Wayne. But subconsciously he emulated the ancient Eastern philosophers, and dug that deep well in carpentry, like the ferryman did in his lifetime of ferrying passengers in Hesse's *Siddhartha*, like Julia Child with her lifetime as a chef, and like my two favorites of all time, Click and Clack with their auto mechanics. Tiger said that the Gautama Buddha sat and meditated under the Bodhi tree for forty-nine days straight, without getting up, before attaining enlightenment. I could not sit still long enough to dig a deep well, or so I thought. It never occurred to me that carpentry was the one deep well that I had been digging since childhood and would continue to dig after Princeton. I was clumsy and disorganized; I accidentally snipped off my left thumb with an electric saw at sixteen. I've been especially careful with saws ever since then, but I constantly trip over extension cords, drop things, and generally maintain my jobsites in a state of chaos.

Look all around you as we begin,
But there is no cause for alarm.
I'm building a house for you to live in,
From the lumber strewn in your yard.

I was a clumsy child, but I was a quick study when it came to carpentry. And I emulated my father, who started teaching me at an early age. I had a scholarship and financial aid at Princeton, but it didn't cover the incidentals that a college student might require, such as regular trips to my grandparents in Camden, or to my parents in Bridgeview, to get my pasta fix. Princeton had the Annex, a basement-Italian restaurant-pub right across Nassau Street from campus, which could pinch-hit for my Nonna (grandmother) in an emergency. But she had a much wider repertoire—homemade Orecchiette, Veal Scallopini, Veal Marsala, the real homemade meatballs—that don't bounce, brasciole (every family had their own secret recipe), Calamari, Vongole, Melanzane and this is really making me hungry.

Fortunately, I had a steady stream of little repair jobs, mainly fixing damaged walls, doors, windows, and furniture at the Prospect Avenue eating clubs, after their weekend parties. Built in the late 1800's through the early 1900's, they had the look and size of opulent mansions, in a variety of styles, including Tudor, Queen Anne, Gothic, Edwardian and Colonial Revival. Lucky for me, they needed constant upkeep.

By the time I graduated, I had a backlog of work to do for professors and townsfolk as well. Our plan, which obviously never materialized, was for me to continue with my carpentry projects, while Mary would attend graduate school at Princeton. Then I would go to graduate school, but only if I could decide what I wanted to study. So I just fell into carpentry without having any real plan to do that or anything else. And I have been content to stay with it all these years. Now where was I?

Little moth, circling back to the kitchen encounter, after assuring the readers that there will be absolutely no more digressions, with antennae hunkered down like furrowed brows, in deep thought: "Wait a minute. They weren't horses; they were plates. And they were spinning, in the nightmare I had over and over the whole time I was at Princeton. I was some sort of juggler on a stage, spinning plates on these tall sticks. There were dozens of sticks with plates spinning on them. And I had to run all over the stage to keep them spinning, except more kept appearing out of nowhere. And I got more and more frantic, trying to keep them spinning, until they all came crashing down, and I was laughed at and booed off the stage."

Big Moth, with antennae the size of two TV towers wiggling all over the place: "Joseph, those weren't plates crashing. Your horses were stampeding out of the corral, where they could roam free on the wide prairie. That's the true meaning of an unbridled mind—while not necessarily an unbridled genius. Your thoughts will never walk in calm circles, let alone in straight lines, but out on the prairie they can see beautiful vistas, and they have a lot more elbow room."

Little moth, shivering from the wind Big Moth created, when his Concorde-sized wings started fluttering in preparation for takeoff: "Hey! Hey! One more question. Am I really that clumsy, or were you doing it?"

Big Moth, speaking thunderously, over the FLUB-BUB-BUB-BUB of his wings: "Joseph, when Mary criticized you for driving like Mr. Magoo, I thought, if only he could drive that *well*."

Although it happened about ten years ago, I remember it like it was yesterday. Our conversation seemed to have lasted for hours. But it was at the speed of light, in dimensions of reality that the string theorists recently discovered, where a thousand angels can not only stand on the head of a pin; they can spread out and do the Macarena, without getting their arms and legs tangled. He told me much more than I've told you so far, but I have to weave in the rest of his words like a fine gold thread purposely hidden in a seemingly worthless tapestry. God's words are not ineffable. But, to paraphrase Nietzsche, they're like a refreshing, ice-cold spring that nevertheless should be entered slowly.

Jonah in the Spaceship Episode

I am stunned, but I want to be stunned, since I have sworn to you, my soul, to trust you even if you lead me through madness . . . It is unquestionable: if you enter into the world of the soul, you are like a madman, and a doctor would consider you to be sick.

— Carl Jung

GOD NEVER CAME RIGHT OUT AND TOLD ME TO SHARE this. But he was dropping non-verbal hints all over the place. The whole time we were having our non-verbal conversation, one facet of his left compound gypsy moth eye kept staring right out of the dining room window at the dinghy in my driveway, as if to say, "You better share this, or you could end up like Jonah."

I raised my gypsy moth wings in an almost imperceptible sigh of exasperation, which said in no uncertain terms, "You idiot, there are no whales in Saint Augustine." For as long as I can remember, Tiger and I have taken the dinghy out in Saint Augustine's Matanzas Bay for blue crabs almost every weekend. You can catch them most of the year around here. I don't mean to digress, except to show that I know my local waters pretty well. And I have never seen a whale around here. We have some pretty big sharks on occasion.

(Tiger's brain injury from the car accident left him unable to speak or write. But in some activities, such as eating or walking, he is able to function, albeit at a slow pace. Even then, I have to push him. He'd prefer to just sit all the time.)

Mr. Big Moth gave me an almost indiscernible, but steely-eyed glance, the kind poker players use when they're bluffing, that said, "Whatever. Right whales come by here every winter. I myself wrote the genetic code that makes them do it year in and year out. I could slip one through the inlet at high tide, have him swallow you and take you out to sea before you knew what hit you. But if you insist that I'm bluffing, I could put you in a pretty big shark."

I was visibly shaken, because I had just grabbed a life preserver that happened to be made of lead. But since I fret and fidget all the time, I hoped he wouldn't notice. My compound eyes peered all around searchingly, as if to say, "How about a spaceship? Aren't you omnipotent and omniscient? Can't you put me in a spaceship?" And after a little hesitation, "Alright then, alright then, I'll share it. But as you can surely imagine, it will take someone like me a long time to gather my thoughts."

That's how I survived at Princeton. If you can't make sense, then you'd better be well versed in the subtle application of logical fallacies. This is the *argumentum ad egotism* trick, the appeal to his ego. I'm sure we settled on a spaceship, but my recollection about that isn't clear.

Oops, some of my young foal readers' legs are starting to

wobble on this one. "If your memory isn't clear to *you*," they ask, "then how can *we* trust it?" And the jaded-old-gelding and old-gray-mare readers are sounding a chorus of cynicism, echoing Thurber's cartoon character's middle-aged wife, who, aroused from her sound sleep, said, "All right, have it your way—you heard a seal bark."

"All Right, Have It Your Way—You Heard a Seal Bark!"

No worries. I assure you that everything I say came straight from the horse's mouth. It's 20/20, on the mark, and surgically precise. I won't go so far as to say that God is speaking it through me. Although I feel like a human Ouija board at times, that may be a symptom of some other ailment.

And jc is his messenger. I use small case letters, so you

won't confuse him with other, more notable J.C.'s of the past, such as Joan Crawford, Julius Caesar, Jesus Christ, Julia Child, Jimmy Carter, Jim Carrey and of course my two all-time favorites, Johnny Carson and Johnny Cash. My jc stands for *jump-up comedian*, a suitable sobriquet for the heart, or the inner voice, as some call it. My father was a jump-up comedian. He was generally a quiet man. But sometimes, at a family gathering, or even in church, he'd jump up and say something ridiculous.

"Joey," he said, "you know what the priest is saying?" He was asking me right in the middle of the church service, which was in Latin then.

I was ten. I said, "Dad, shhhhh! We'll get in trouble." My voice was quivering and my hair was sticking straight up, partly from the "Butch Hair Wax" my parents made me use on my crew cut, and partly because I still hadn't figured out when to sit, stand or kneel, and I expected the priest to single me out for it at any moment. He'd punctuate his reading of the Gospel in Latin with, "That boy's an idiot. Sister Frances, get him out of here. Isn't he in your confirmation class?" Then he'd continue reading without skipping a beat. I would be pulled out of the pew by Sister Frances and dragged out of the sanctuary by my ear.

My father would continue, just slightly more muted. (He had a low voice like a frog. It's hard for a voice like that to whisper.) "The priest says, 'Sisters pass the biscuits please.'" My father sang it with a long note held on ple-e-e-e-ease. "And the nuns in the balcony reply, 'Sorry there are no mo-o-o-o-o-ore,'" which he sang in the highest voice he could muster. I tried to conceal my laughter, but snot was coming out of my nose from the combination with my extreme fright. I named jc after the nickname I gave my father. His real name was Giacobbe, Italian for Jacob.

The soul's journey is not in space or time.
It's hard to follow with our finite minds.
The heart knows the way and acts as our guide.

But everything jc says sounds so ridiculous at first, he reminds me of my father. "Joseph, you and God will be collaborators on what Thomas Mann called 'literature's ideal...a perfect equilibrium between jest and high seriousness.' You'll be the perfect comic relief for God's high seriousness. He'll provide the living waters, and you'll add the flavoring and food coloring to make them palatable. He'll provide the meat to eat that they know not of, and you'll cover it with delicious sauces like they do in France. Man's soul needs a teaspoon or two of castor oil, and God chose you to hide it in a bowl of Lucky Charms. Besides, God can reach a wider audience with a work of fiction, and you live in a fictional world."

I started to write a thoughtful treatise, in the systematic style of Immanuel Kant, titled, "Critique of the Soul." But jc said, "Joseph, you can't put new wine in an old wineskin. The old cisterns are broken and won't hold water. You're not speaking to the readers' minds; you're speaking to their souls. Don't try to corral your horses. Hook them up to a cart and take your readers out for a ride."

Psychologists say that we use only one tenth of our mind. Of course you know they're wrong. They should say that we *control* a tenth of it. The other nine tenths are out of control, but they work all the time. This book is about the nine tenths of the mind that we don't control.

Psychologists caught a glimpse of the subconscious when they said that dreams are closer to our true nature than our conscious state. But they would have us believe that the mind is like a house, and dreams give us a glimpse through the keyhole. In *their* scenario, our conscious thoughts sit calmly out on the front porch in their Sunday best and wave to passers-by, while inside the house our subconscious thoughts are jumping all around like the three stooges on Pogo Sticks and acting crazy.

Don't believe everything psychologists say. I can tell you from firsthand experience that our subconscious thoughts wouldn't stand for being cooped up in the house all the time. They need wide open spaces. They like to sleep under the stars. If they want to jump around like the three stooges on Pogo Sticks, there's plenty more room out on the prairie for that sort of stuff. In *my* scenario, dreams do give us a glimpse of the subconscious, but they do it by waiting for us to fall asleep, then hitching some of our horses to a cart and taking us for an all-night hayride in our pajamas.

Being half-asleep and running around in the dark, we rarely remember what we saw. And if we do, it's usually because we were scared half out of our wits. To make matters worse, dreams generally steal our pajamas, just before depositing us, for some inexplicable reason, out in the middle of the prairie, in the driver's seat of a convertible, with the top down in the rain, with a wild lion in the passenger seat, and with our children (or our unfinished novel, if we don't have real children) in the back seat. No wonder we wake up every morning in bed with a stranger, even when we sleep alone. We know only one tenth of ourselves.

Not to worry; this book will make the prairie your home. If you are ready to follow Socrates' (also Thales') maxim to "know thyself," then you should get a firm grip on this book with both hands, because we're about to go on a similar hayride. But this time you'll be wide awake and out in broad daylight. In no time you'll know every verdant meadow and wooded glen, every babbling brook and scenic overlook, every pond, glade and thicket like the back of your hand.

> *One pays lip service to self-knowledge, but is terrified by it and resists it.*

> — Walter Kaufmann

Before we begin, let me make a few prefatory remarks to make our hayride more comfortable. Those readers who have ever tried to "harness" their subconscious will find this section easy, because they already know it's full of wild horses. Let me just point out to the others that your mind and your soul are going to have vastly different perspectives. Your conscious mind is forced to conform to a convoluted habitat, the cerebral cortex. I don't know why God insists on calling it a corral. It's closer in appearance to the famous labyrinth at Notre-Dame de Chartres, or to those maze-like stockades that cows run through at the livestock auctions.

Your subconscious mind is like a prairie, though. Not only does nine tenths of your mind make its home there, but your soul lives there too. Everybody and his brother wrote a book to help you find your soul, such as Jung's *Modern Man in Search of a Soul*, Moore's *Care of the Soul*, Hillman's *The Soul's Code*, Zukav's *The Seat of the Soul*, Canfield's *Chicken Soup for the Soul*, and Thiele's *Friedrich Nietzsche and the Politics of the Soul*. Jung said that as infinitely hard as it would be for a Christian to imitate Christ, for a Jew to imitate the Baal Shem Tov, or for a Buddhist to imitate the Buddha, it was even harder to be who *you* are. The Tao says, "True perfection in man is not perfect, but perfectly himself."

They all suggest that you "harness" your horses. That sounds good in theory, but it won't work in practice. As the expert in the "field" most familiar with the territory, I'm here to help you learn the ways of the great Roman circus riders, the desultors, who jumped from horse to horse. You have to trust your horses to take you where you want to go. Animals do some things better than humans. Shakespeare was fond of comparing us to beasts, but Dostoevsky hit the nail on the head when he said we were far lower in some respects. So, if my writing seems desultory to your convoluted mind, it will make perfect sense to your soul. In Shakespeare's words, "Tho this be madness, yet there is method in't."

To your mind, my writing will seem to follow the path your lawnmower would make through your yard if it were hitched up to the tail of a bucking bronco. But your soul will see neat rows, mowed first from front to back, then crisscrossed from side to side for extra measure, the hedges neatly trimmed, the sidewalk edged, and all the flower beds carefully weeded and mulched.

Your mind will think it's eating one of those scrambled, scattered, smothered, covered, and diced meals they serve at restaurants along the highways, or worse, the gross regurgitation and eructation of partially digested food that birds feed to their young. But your soul will taste it reconstituted into a gourmet meal, with soup, salad, appetizer, entrée, sorbet to refresh the palate, dessert, and of course, the savory course.

Your mind will see the Sagrada Familia cathedral, the epitome of the "more is not less" school of architecture, with its chaotic juxtaposition of architectural elements, its dripping ornamentation so excessive that a new word had to be invented to describe it, "gaudy," named after its famed architect, Antonio Gaudi. But your soul sees the epitome of the "less is more" school, a Bauhaus office building, where form not only follows function, but every aesthetic element serves not one, but several simultaneous functions.

Your mind hears an excruciatingly loud, if not downright psychotic, electric guitar riff by Led Zeppelin or Jimi Hendrix. But your soul hears a heavenly symphony. Every note is in its proper place, and not a chord is wasted. The main theme is left momentarily for a divertimento that enriches its meaning in a way that seems not only necessary, but divinely inspired, before returning to coda for a brief reinforcement, and then finally a thunderous recapitulation, followed by the inevitable standing ovation. Sorry I got a little carried away. I promise it won't happen again. In a nutshell, your mind really will hear a seal barking, but your soul will cry, "It is the voice of a God, and not of a man," like they said about Herod.

Let your soul be your pilot. — Sting

Those skittish readers, who are about to dart from the book like a hart from the brook, should take a short intermission to contemplate Confucius' analect, "Why contemplate beyond death, when you don't even know life, God when you don't know man, man when you won't even look at yourself?" I'll impose one more digression—a brief divertimento—on the rambunctious readers to give the skittish readers time to mosey on out of the stables.

This is not really an imposition. Digressions are like speed bumps, meant to slow the speed-readers down, so they don't miss something important. Some of you are chomping at the bit, anxious to get out on the track and race to the finish line. Digressions help you pause a moment to get your bearings, so you don't run in the wrong direction. And they give the skittish readers a minute or two to make their way to the starting gate. I don't want to sound preachy, but some readers won't believe anything a madman says. So for celebrity endorsements, I'll just note that the main purpose of Dante's "Intermezzo," Goethe's "Walpurgis Night" and Dostoevsky's "Grand Inquisitor" was to slow you down. Those of you who are already familiar with Jonathan Swift's "Digression in Praise of Digressions" shouldn't need celebrity endorsements.

The Publisher Episode
– A Divertimento

(I admit it. This episode reads like an excruciating electric guitar riff, but with language as the instrument. I promise it won't happen again. The glossary at the end mostly pertains to this episode.)

> *Inspiration...occurs in the form of being-beside-oneself, a theia mania—hence that inspiration likewise appears to "the multitude" as madness.*

> — Josef Pieper

HEROD GOT IN A LOT OF TROUBLE WHEN HE TOOK undeserved credit for sounding like God. The horses should get the credit for my words. And jc is my poor excuse for a muse. I shouldn't have to tell you that jc and I argue all the time. He almost got me put in jail for murder. He said, "Joseph, go to the publishing houses of New York, and take neither gold, nor silver, nor scrip for the trip, and take no thought how or what you shall speak."

I said, "Hold your horses, you idiot. Don't you realize that I'm a colt writer making his first whinny?"

"Joseph," he said, "How do you expect your readers to trust *their* hearts, if you don't practice what you preach by trusting your own heart?"

Following jc's advice, I took a pleasant train ride to New York. (That's a bald-faced lie. I assure you it will never happen again; jc had to drag me, as the saying goes, kicking and screaming all the way to New York.) As I approached the publisher's building, I saw two security guards smoking cigarettes by the entrance. Again, on the advice of jc, I retraced my steps back a block and a half to a small office supply store, where I bought a sheet of poster board and an inexpensive tripod easel. Then, after borrowing a thick black marker from the salesclerk, I wrote in large letters, "CAUTION: DO NOT MOON THE WINDOW CLEANERS."

After convincing the publishing house security guards that I worked with the window cleaners, I found myself in the twenty-fifth floor, bookcase-lined, burled walnut-paneled, antique-adorned, innermost and uppermost chamber of the Temple of the Publishing Gods, in the office of the Editor Emeritus, where I came upon a very elderly, father-figure gentleman at his desk, who was nodding his head to sleep, in tune it seemed, to the tranquil melody of Satie's Gymnopedies, whose piped-in sound had accompanied me all the way from the ground floor to his office on the top floor, making my ascent up the elevator, under the circumstances, seem like I was rising calmly and peacefully into the heavens.

"A madman?" he asked, only slightly startled. "Ah, sit down, son." And while I sat gazing over his shoulders at the New York skyline out his window, he launched into a nostalgically enthused, but somnolently subdued discussion of the fictional madmen that had been, in long years past, masterfully imbued with life by Gogol, Balzac, Dostoevsky, Beckett and many others.

I admit that we really haven't gotten out of the corral yet. You have to allow a little more time than usual for a madman to gather his thoughts. Plato said, "...the greatest of blessings come to us through madness" (*Phaedrus* 244a). His *Theia Mania* or "divine madness," the madness of poets, oracles, prophets, and seers, soared *above* reason. And he warned that our words would flow out of us with no restraint, like water from a fountain (Laws 719c). Plato is known for his understatements. It's more like a roaring freak storm than water from a fountain, a roaring freak storm that's flibberty-gibberty and far from the norm, springing forth until the forest is filled with water and a river runs through the desert. (Plato got the idea from *Isaiah*.) So you can imagine that the act of gathering my thoughts is somewhat akin to herding rain drops in a thunderstorm, or more precisely, in a hurricane.

Unfortunately, while at the publisher, I was crudely mistaken for a case of organic madness, which Plato said was *below* reason, because, during the course of our quiet encounter, the kind that often takes place between a novitiate and his elder mentor—that almost clichéd sequence of expatiation, remonstration, expostulation, and finally the inevitable superfetation of mutual proclamations of admiration—oops, forgive me. I need a strong compass and some good charts to keep my thoughts on course. Oh yes, because a minor saliva spray, possibly due to madness, or to my misaligned jaw from the car accident, may have accompanied my speech, while answering, "But those other madmen were fictional; I am real. Whoever touches this book touches a madman (echoing Whitman, who in turn was echoing Bernini). Be still and know that I am mad (echoing God)."

Okay. So I got a little carried away, especially when I yelled, for dramatic effect, "ECCE LOONO" (behold the lunatic), echoing Nietzsche's *Ecce Homo* (behold the man), which in turn echoes Pontius Pilate's "Ecce Homo," while he pointed at Jesus. Madmen get carried away all the time, sometimes literally.

Just like at that very moment, when I was jarred from one of my occasional episodes of unintentional prosopopoeia—a stage device, where the actor speaks with an imaginary, deceased, or otherwise absent person—where I get so absorbed in conversation that I don't notice that I'm the only one in it, and saw that I was being levitated, in a manner of speaking, down the hall by the two security guards, who carried me by the shoulders, with my feet floating about six inches above the floor, behind some bumptious, corporate busybody of a baton-twirling, parade-marshal, publishing-industry bureaucrat, who usurped my placard-and-easel prop for his own starring role in our present roving spectacle, which seemed to announce to all onlookers that they would be pilloried and paraded just like me, if they were caught mooning the window cleaners. As I said, the placard was jc's idea. It would not have been so suspicious fifty years ago. He's full of anachronisms.

My escorts could not discern the gentle mood of senescent hebetude that pervaded my mentor's and my harmonious colloquy. In other words, they could not see beyond the diaphanous veil of the natural rise and fall of our barely audible conversational tone, which bore a close mimesis to the musical form. In a nutshell, they could not tell the obvious difference between Cesar Franck's "Sonata in A Major", on the one hand, where the angelically exquisite violin first pleads with you, over and over, to hear how beautiful she sounds, how muliebrious and melodious the voice is that echoes from her innermost being, softly at first, but after you reject her barely audible entreaties repeatedly, she finally rises in an impassioned deliquious crescendo that threatens you with a chainsaw, but you're not alarmed, because you know she's just kidding; and Bartok's "First String Quartet", on the other hand, where all four instruments at once do in fact violently hack you to shreds with machetes throughout the entire song.

I had no idea that the dear editor emeritus was dead. I should have noticed. The third insight in *The Celestine Prophecy* says that we can rearrange the universe in accordance with our expectations. That's quite an exaggeration. More often than not, the universe rearranges us in accordance with *its* expectations. But for fleeting moments it appears to be the other way around. When I got off the elevator and saw "Publisher / Editor Emeritus" on his door, I had such an overwhelming expectation that my book would get a friendly reception, that the universe appeared to rearrange itself accordingly, but in fact it hadn't.

I was released from jail after a few days, when the coroner finally concluded from the autopsy that the editor had died from a heart attack the day before I arrived in New York. Editors are known for sometimes holing up in their office for days, when a can't-put-down read flies over their transom.

His grieving children, who had by now pored through my book, hoping at first to find clues about my motive for murdering their father, escorted me from the precinct house back to their office. And hoping against all odds that I really had a conversation with their father, or with his ghost at least, they gave my book the friendly reception that I expected, or rather I should say that jc expected.

I shouldn't refer to them as children, but after such a close, albeit short-lived friendship with their father, I thought of them as children. I felt paternal toward them. It was as though fate brought me there to be a surrogate for the father they had just lost. The son had his father's Adam's apple, and both he and the daughter had their father's long nose. I have a long nose, which probably reminded them of their father. They were both about my age, perhaps even a little older. But they were so kind and deferential that I saw right away how they perceived me as a father figure.

"Now Mr. Colocento, please don't take offense, but you're aware that your book really *does* appear to have been written by a madman?" the daughter asked.

"It's a dreamlike book," the son added.

"Your father and I were saying the very same thing," I said, "and he agreed, at least I think he agreed, that in Jungian terms, just as the dreams of an individual compensate for his neuroses, so the dreamlike quality of a work of art wrought by a madman could compensate for the collective neuroses of a whole society. It's a great observation on your part; you remind me so much of your father. You hold in your hands what Freud said no one could tell, and what Poe said would make a revolutionary book—the whole truth about oneself."

Freud said that Nietzsche knew more about himself than anyone "who ever lived or was ever likely to live." Freud is known for his overgeneralizations.

Nietzsche's *Ecce Homo* was subtitled "how to become what one is," which in my day would have read as "how to find yourself." But Nietzsche had only *half* of the equation. He said to note the qualities that you *admire* in others, and you would find yourself in those. I discovered the other half of the equation serendipitously, when I sought help at a Codependents Anonymous (CODA) meeting to help me cope with God's seemingly codependent behavior (notwithstanding jc's ridiculous assertion that I was projecting my own codependency onto God).

CODA says to note the qualities that you *don't admire* in others, and you would find yourself in those. They have many ways of emphasizing this, such as, "If you spot it, you got it; if you point a finger, you have three pointing back; and BLAME is an acronym that means 'Better Look At ME.'" That was part of their fourth step. I didn't take their fourth step, because I was carried out of there when I refused to take their third step. The third step said, "We made a decision to turn our will and our lives over to the care of God as we understood him."

"You *idiots*," I screamed, "He's codependent! That's exactly what he *wants* us to do." According to CODA's ninth step I really owe those people an apology for disrupting their meeting. But they have a restraining order, so I can't go back there. Of course I didn't tell the editor's children about the restraining order. They were already upset about their father's death, and I didn't want them to worry about their surrogate father as well. Now let's go on that hayride I promised you. Hold onto your saddles, cowgirls and cowboys.

The Puppy-Face, Challah Loaf, and Hurricane Episode

(Readers familiar with advanced recombinant literary engineering will recognize this as three separate episodes combined into one pretzel-shaped episode. It was not intentional.)

> *There are three infallible ways of pleasing an author, and they form a rising scale of compliment: 1, to tell him you have read one of his books; 2, to tell him you have read all of his books; 3, to ask him to let you read the manuscript of his forthcoming book.*

— Mark Twain

MARK TWAIN'S REMARKS SUGGEST THAT HE AND I share a similar fatherly pride about our writing. The epigenesis of this *oeuvre* was very much like that of a living being. Those readers who share my etymological enthusiasm will quickly recognize that *oeuvre* comes from an earlier French root for oval, which in turn comes from the quintessential oval, the egg. (This is just a wild guess. I have lots of etymological enthusiasm, but no expertise.) And this *oeuvre* proceeded from its subcellular, first-two-word zygote, "My wife..." in that universal, morphological mimicry of phylogenetic evolution, through all the gestational stages, up to and including the beautiful, full-term newborn you so caressingly hold in your arms at this very instant.

Every up-and-coming writer knows what a captive audience a wife can be (Mary embodies this statement more than most). I couldn't wait to show her this new life we would create together. When I visited Mary at her gravesite in New Jersey while the writing was still at this very early stage, I wanted to surprise her, so I began with "small talk" about the latest book I was reading. I told her about Brian Greene's *The Elegant Universe*, and how string theory showed that she could be right beside me in another "parallel" universe, and I wouldn't know it. "At least that's what I think he said," I said.

Then I told her about my latest invention, which I named after her, the *Mary Colocento Challah Loaf Hurricane Prevention System*. These are concrete jetties that I hope to build up and down the coasts of Florida.

If I could digress one last time, I should probably take just a moment, for the benefit of some of my more astute readers who might want to invest in it, to tell you more about this invention. The jetties are shaped like giant challah loaves, which are uniquely designed (probably by You-Know-Who, and he was just waiting for someone to see this application) to have a "wave canceling effect." On second thought, they probably won't stop the hurricanes, but they will stop the storm surge. When the waves hit the challah loaves, the waves disappear. It's all derived from well-known facts about wave cancellation theory and fluid dynamics, similar to what happened in the double slit light experiment.

One or two ingenuous readers might ask, "Where on earth did you get this idea?" The answer is quite simple. The challah loaf is very dear to my *heart*, because it was such an important part of Mary's life. Its shape, though, is remarkably similar to my *mind*. The study of fluid dynamics and other non-linear systems has spawned a relatively young branch of knowledge that I may have mentioned earlier, Chaos Theory—also called the science of complexity or non-linear dynamics—which says that very complex systems, while appearing on the surface to be in total chaos, are found, upon further examination, to have deep structures, feedback loops, "strange attractors" (my personal favorite), recursive symmetries and so forth. That describes my *entire* mind, and your *subconscious* mind, in a nutshell. It appears to be all twisted in knots like a challah loaf, but it's actually just a very complex system.

As an aside I should mention that Mary's junior thesis at Princeton, *Chaos Theory and the Marginalia in the Talmud*, found that while the marginalia appeared at first glance to be in total chaos, upon further study they were found to contain an attribute that she thought was unique to them--perfect *thought-spirals*, in addition to all the classical attributes of non-linear systems. Still, she thought that the marginalia could certainly benefit from a woman's touch. She just wanted to tidy them up a bit.

I had never heard of chaos theory until I met Mary. We met in March of 1977, in the spring of our junior year of college.

The challah loaf is static. But the subconscious mind is dynamic. And dynamic systems, when allowed to follow their course, eventually reach a point in time—the *bifurcation* point, when they suddenly reorganize themselves on a higher level, sort of like a traffic jam that starts moving again. I stole that example from Mary's thesis. I promise it won't happen again. The most stunning examples she wrote about were, on a molecular scale: the Belousov-Zhabotinskii reaction, where an apparently chaotic mixture of molecules in a petri dish suddenly organizes itself into a perfect ring, which pulsates before your eyes and spreads out from the center; and on a cosmic scale: Hoag's Object, a galaxy that at some point in its multi-billion-year history was organized into a perfect ring.

As you read this book, your brain tissue is actually taking part in the first in-vivo Belousov-Zhabotinskii reaction. What appears as a series of fragmentary episodes to your conscious mind is slowly becoming a series of connected dots in your subconscious. Studies of autism and savantism suggest that people with those conditions rely more on non-linear than linear thought processes. There is a corollary, that people without those conditions are locked out of non-linear thought processes, or that they try to force linearity on non-linear processes. They fear the apparent chaos of the non-linear and mistake it for madness. The Tao anticipated Chaos Theory when it said, "Do you have the patience to wait until the mud settles and the water is clear?"

That God would allow me of all people to invent the *Mary Colocento Challah Loaf Hurricane Prevention System* can only be attributed to some divine sense of poetic justice, because my mind probably has more in common with the challah loaf *and* with the hurricane than anyone's on the planet. If some of my timid readers need encouragement to get out their checkbooks and make an investment—the project is ready-to-go, shovel-ready in construction parlance, pending funding—what I'm about to tell you would be considered a "sign" in theological circles.

The hurricane is the most ubiquitous shape in the universe. From a distance, our own galaxy, the Milky Way, looks like a hurricane. That's why your tub drains the way it does, and why God himself talks in spirals. That's why you can solve very hard problems only by *brainstorming*. I mostly talk in circles, but occasionally, on a good day, I find that I *can* talk in spirals. If you want to get in on the ground floor of something whose time has come, this is the perfect opportunity. I told you this would take just a moment of your time.

Sometimes I get so beside myself with asides that I end up miles away, and I have to use set theory to wend my way back to the central discussion. Out here on the prairie we call it "marking the trail." But at last we've arrived.

(This is a perfect example of non-linear thought, which is much more powerful than linear thought, in the same way that non-linear equations in math are more powerful than linear equations. This book is just the tip of the iceberg of non-linear thought that goes on beneath the surface in all of you, all the time. In fact, at this very minute, while your mind is grunting and making faces, while trying to follow along, your soul has probably left your body momentarily to get some refreshments. In trying to grasp his own soul, Jung said, "I limp after you on crutches of understanding. I am a man and you stride like a God.")

Finally, I reached for my wallet and said as nonchalantly as I could, "Oh. I almost forgot I had part of the novel I'm writing in here." (Another lie of omission, I didn't tell her it was the only part I had so far.)

"You're writing a novel?" She seemed surprised.

"Oh," I said, "It's not finished yet. Maybe I shouldn't

show you until it's finished. Isn't it bad luck? But I think I'm supposed to ask for a release or permission or whatever they call it, because as you'll see by the beginning, it's probably going to be mostly about you."

Then I deftly flipped "My wife" out of my wallet with the lightning speed of a card shark. I had been practicing on the train. I could not stop looking at "My wife" all the way up the East Coast, with that preternatural fondness, like Mark Twain's, that only a father could feel.

It was hard to gauge her response; she was mostly just incredulous. The sudden realization that a potentially famous writer stood before her probably hadn't worn off yet. So I just smiled that knowing smile that said, "I knew you'd love it, and rest assured that your adulation will not go unappreciated. I'll probably send a limo for you as soon as it's finished, so you can accompany me on the book tour." With that we both laughed. One of Mary's most endearing qualities is that she always laughs with me, and not at me.

I could hardly sleep after the first page was completed. I spent half the night gazing into its closed, baby chick-embryo eyes. And when I completed my little hairless, puppy-faced first episode, I rewarded myself with another trip to see Mary. On the train I imagined that I might walk it through the graveyard to her on a leash, both of our heads held high, then tilting in unison to a distant horn blast, this prodigiously loyal, prenatal puppy already starting to mimic his master's every idiosyncrasy.

By now I shouldn't have to explain that free association is a double entendre for me, since I don't have to pay a psychiatrist for it. But you can't expect me to jump right out of my spaceship like Michael Rennie in the classic film *The Day the Earth Stood Still* and get shot like he did. First I have to unfurl a few large banners that say, "DON'T

SHOOT...IT'S A GIFT...I COME IN PEACE...I MEAN YOU NO HARM," and so forth. So before we move along, please allow me to pause for a very brief moment to give Mary the credit she's due for her innumerable editorial contributions to my writing.

John Stuart Mill said that he and his wife had so many discussions about everything he wrote that he wasn't sure who should get the credit for his words. I have an awful lot in common with him, but this is particularly apropos, because Mary played a similar role to Mrs. Mill's in the authorship of this book, and she must share much of the credit.

Mary and I had so many discussions throughout the course of my writing, that if train passengers got frequent-flyer miles, I'd have enough by now to get a ride on the space shuttle. These were admittedly one-sided conversations, but I could sense her feelings on everything. I'd sit by her gravestone and polish it with a handkerchief until I could almost see her face in it. And as I read to her, she nodded approvingly, or frowned, as the case warranted, when she caught me in one of the frequent non sequiturs or otherwise convoluted thought processes for which I am justly famous.

All couples have their own special fantasies in which they indulge behind closed doors. Anyone who shared a dorm in college knows that there are plenty of opportunities to be alone with your girlfriend, for example, when your roommate has a class, and you don't. My roommate Tiger had a pair of short, dull edged swords, called butterfly swords, which he used for his Kung Fu demonstrations. I would sometimes chase Mary around our dorm room, brandishing the swords and wearing a bandanna on my head. I was the pirate, and she was my captive maiden.

"Come over here, you little maiden," I'd say in a gravelly voice. "If you try to get away, I'll have you bound and keelhauled."

"Stay away, you meshuganer pirate," she'd say. "Don't come near me."

So you can imagine her smile staring out at me from the granite headstone, as I stood up, brandished my arms about and told her, on a recent visit, "You little landlubber you, all this declension and conjugation nonsense of yours is as confusing as a mass of sargassum, serving no purpose but to clog the writer's rudder. Now, one more word about it and I'll have you bound and keelhauled."

The Lightning Episode

I grew up with great ineptness in the common affairs of everyday life. I was far longer than children generally are before I could put on my clothes. I know not how many years passed before I could tie a knot. My articulation was long imperfect; one letter, r, I could not pronounce until I was nearly sixteen...I was, utterly unobservant: I was, as my father continually told me, like a person who had not the organs of sense: my eyes and ears seemed of no use to me, so little did I see or hear what was before me...I was constantly acquiring bad habits, and never breaking myself of them...and judging and acting like a person devoid of common sense; and which would make me, he said, grow up a mere oddity...and unfit for all the common purposes of life.

— John Stuart Mill

THE QUOTE FROM MILL IS A TYPE OF SHORTHAND THAT allows me to briefly summarize my own childhood, without spending so much time on it that I give the mistaken appearance of being self-preoccupied. (I am so sorry. Another lie of omission. I just can't control myself sometimes. I promise it won't happen again. The quote from Mill summarizes my adulthood as well.) But Mary was a precocious child. She ended up following in the footsteps of her father, a theologian, but she started in the direction of her mother, a paleontologist.

Mary's first attempt at paleontology happened so early in her development, she told me, that it was hard to say whether it was instinct or inclination. As a toddler she accidentally recreated the primordial ooze in her suburban New Jersey backyard, by tipping her dog Darwin's water bowl into the big hole he had dug beside it. By the time she told me this story in college, she could not remember what provoked her to crawl into the hole. "Ah ha! Serendipity," I said.

"No. Propinquity," she said, and that it was more likely the feminine instinct to take a mud bath than leanings in the direction of paleontology. But her mother's frequent phone conversations, dinners and so forth with fellow paleontologists, while holding Mary on her lap, must have had some educational value, because when crawling out of the hole, Mary performed a perfect reenactment of the first creature crawling out of the primordial ooze eons ago, judging from the look on her mother's face, she said.

All through elementary school she made extensive backyard excavations to find the "missing link," about which she had overheard many heated debates at the kitchen table. Darwin shared her deep interest in these backyard excavations. He was a large, black "standard" poodle--a misnomer, since the standard breed is twice as large as other poodles. After several years of close collaboration, long debates and excruciating lucubration, Mary and Darwin had a complete cow skeleton, minus the skull, cleaned and catalogued. As a fifth grader in attendance at one of her parents' dinner parties, where the inevitable "missing link" discussion reared its ugly head, she made the astonishing announcement that man descended from the cow she had painstakingly unearthed in her backyard.

She had one final brush with science and her first brush with God at the same time. It was a stormy afternoon in October of seventh grade, a fateful day, where a seemingly benign impulse is acted upon, and a life's course is irrevocably altered. It was a perfect day for ghosts to preoccupy the mind of a preteen adolescent, or merely to occupy in this instance. "What would *possess* a twelve-year-old, rather refined, somewhat studious, and therefore seemingly mature young lady, other than the ghost of Ben Franklin, to do what I did?" she said.

Seeking a qualified candidate to follow up on his lightning experiments, which Mary had learned about in her science class that very morning, he must have settled on her. She said it was an eerily unexplainable, sudden impulse of experimentation, of the kind found in the Catholic Church's age-old annals on possession, transmogrification, and exorcism, as well as in the short stories of Isaac Bashevis Singer, one of her favorite authors. She disassembled the floor-to-ceiling, spring-loaded, brass-plated, nickel and steel alloy pole lamp, the kind that was popular back then, that stood beside her father's easy chair, and stood it up in one of Darwin's deepest backyard excavations, right in the middle of a severe thunderstorm.

"A *katastrofe!*" That's what the yard looked like after the lightning struck. Those were her words when she described it to me.

"A what?" I said.

"That's Yiddish for catastrophe, a huge mess," she said. "It was like a bomb went off in the dirt; the whole back of our house was covered in mud, and some of the neighbors' houses too."

She was very fortunate, escaping with barely a scratch. Darwin was declared a local hero for digging himself and her out from several feet of muddy dirt. He was buried with her in the explosion, because he started to drag her away by her dress sleeves from the impending doom moments before the lightning struck. Animals have a sixth sense in these situations.

This recovery operation was witnessed in its entirety by an elderly neighbor who watched from his shattered kitchen window. Every neighbor's windows in the direct path of the air shock for three houses back in all directions were shattered. The retired neighbor looked out after hearing the noise, which he described as louder than the dynamiting he heard on the Panama Canal construction, where he worked years ago. I hope I'm not repeating myself; I seem to remember saying something about the Panama Canal earlier. But I do remember asking her if this second mud bath showed that she did in fact have that propensity for mud baths that she mentioned earlier.

She described it as a near-death, white-light experience, and chthonic in a literal sense, in which God appeared to her, saying, "Mary, why don't you try following in your father's footsteps, instead of your mother's? You're just not cut out to be a scientist." (During our kitchen encounter I asked God if this was another violation of the rules. He said she may have confused her own heart's inner voice with his, especially when compounded with the bright flash of lightning.) The only permanent effect she suffered, other than changing her career goals, was that the retinal cells directly behind her pupils were caramelized by the intensity of the lightning flash. She could see fine, she said, but not stereoscopically well enough to drive.

But didn't I mention earlier that there's a silver lining for every cloud, because those caramelized nerve endings reflected light in a way that made her eyes so radiant that they seemed divine. The bizarre side effect was that her eyes aimed at the other person's shoulder when she was really looking straight at them, so that people in conversation with her were forever brushing phantom dandruff off their shoulders. And some thought the look in her eyes was from madness, and not the result of a bizarre accident. That's possibly what drew me to her in the first place.

The Princeton Episode

BUCOLIC, PASTORAL, GOTHIC-BELL-TOWERED Princeton. I'm pretty sure I went there. I seem to remember that it was the only school that would take me. When I was there, it was the epicenter of reason *and* madness in the universe. And I dare say, they couldn't tell us apart. The gentleman's "C" had long ago disappeared, but they still had the "C" for "crazy." That was when the professor couldn't make sense of your paper. But he wasn't sure if your work was so far "up there" that you deserved an A, or so far "out there" that you deserved an F.

Tiger was my dormitory roommate and closest friend all through college. But it didn't start out that way. We were assigned to a dorm together in our freshman year. Princeton's dorms were like rooms in a medieval castle, with heavy, dark-stained woodwork. I was sitting on a window seat in our room, looking out from the opened, leaded-glass casement windows at the stone walls and late summer greenery three stories below, when Tiger walked in. Tiger was carrying a gym bag with several swords and other assorted Kung Fu weaponry hanging out of it. He started toward me with one hand out and the other still clutching the bag. He was introducing himself, "Yu Chin, Yeung Yu Chin." But I had a sneaking suspicion that he didn't like my chin and he was going to use one of the swords to cut it off.

I have never been suicidal. But my medical record still shows that in 1974, during freshman orientation week at Princeton, I was taken to the McCosh Hall infirmary for observation because of an attempted suicide. A group of other freshmen who had gathered in the courtyard below reported me to campus security. They were concerned. They had been "warned" earlier that week by an ever-so-helpful, senior-class tour guide that Princeton had a lot of students leaping out windows, because the work was so hard.

I stood up on the window seat and was inching closer and closer to the open window to get a better look for something below it to cushion my flight to safety. Thank God Tiger was so adept at his "sport"—he called it, because had he not made it across the room so fast to grab me by the arm, I would have jumped from the sheer fright of seeing him rushing toward me. He was trying to save me, I learned after regaining my composure.

By the time I got out of the infirmary several days later, Tiger's constant visits to show his concern had already cemented our friendship. It wasn't very long after that before he started referring to me as the embodiment of the Confucian saying—I think it's called an analect—that rotten wood cannot be carved, nor can dung walls be plastered. And I nicknamed him Tiger, partly—as I may have said already, because he was ferocious and stealthy, partly because it was our school's mascot--the word must have been flying around in my head (in circles, obviously), and partly because in the Italian-American neighborhood in

Camden, New Jersey, where I grew up, everyone had to have a nickname. And a lot of thought went into them. I witnessed the vigorous debate that went into my nickname one day in fourth grade in the school cafeteria. First someone suggested Pinocchio, because I had an unusually long nose even for an Italian. But fortunately it got finessed by an all-wise sixth grader, whose father was "connected," into *Joey Nostrils*.

Our friendship has always been on a par with the great friendships throughout history, starting in prehistoric times with Fred Flintstone & Barney Rubble, then David & Jonathan in the *Old Testament*, and up through modern times with Twain's Tom Sawyer & Huck Finn, Hesse's Narcissus & Goldman, Steinbeck's George & Lennie, and TV's Laurel & Hardy, Abbot & Costello, and finally Ralph Kramden & Ed Norton.

Of course there is an exception for every rule. In our case it was when he tried to teach me Kung Fu. For one Christmas in elementary school—I can't remember which one—my parents (aka Santa) gave me an inflatable Popeye punching bag, the kind that had sand in the bottom, so it bounced back up when you knocked it down. This is the sort of friendship Tiger and I had during my introduction to Kung Fu, except that Tiger was Popeye throwing the punches at me. I was Wimpy's friend, the big-nosed, mad-scientist Professor Wotasnozzle, and I didn't bounce back up.

That was how it ended when he introduced me to the Chi Sau. This is a Kung Fu exercise where you stand facing an opponent with both arms outstretched, but just partially, sort of like stretched-out-but-still-noticeably-bent chicken wings. The hands are straight out, in line with the forearms. But there's a twist. One arm has the elbow pointing up and the opposite arm has the elbow pointing down. The opponent's arms are in the same position, but as mirror images of yours, so his arm with elbow pointing down is on the same side of you as your arm with elbow pointing up. The sides of your hands are lightly touching the sides of the opponent's hands.

Now you both rotate your elbows in an outward arc, so that your elbow that was pointing down is now pointing up, and vice versa. Your hands remain in light contact with the opponent's for the entire exercise. So imagine, my right arm has the elbow pointing down and my right forearm and outstretched hand pointing up, not straight up, but sort of a shallow diagonal. As my right elbow rotates outward and up, my right forearm rotates inward and down. My left arm is doing the opposite. The opponent's arms are doing the same rotations, but with the arm on the same side as mine rotating his elbow down when mine's rotating up. And you do this over and over until you get into a smooth rhythm. From a distance it would look like the two of you were rocking an invisible baby in an odd-shaped invisible basket in synchrony.

Then BUHHHH! FUHHHH! The first sound is Tiger's palm or fist or whatever it was, suddenly and seemingly out of nowhere, hitting me in the chest so hard that it knocked me across the room. The second sound was the wind being knocked out of me with the speed and force equal to, but in the opposite direction of me flying across the room. Eventually, I'm supposed to develop some sort of sensitivity in my hand so that even blindfolded, I would anticipate his sudden, inexplicable urge to kill me and be able to counter it with an equal but opposite force. The fatal flaw with that idea was that my arms were about half the diameter of Tiger's arms. He wanted me to fight way above my weight class. That is why I made it clear, *very* clear that he would have to find another Chi Sau partner. I may have gone so far as to invent a hit-man cousin Vito with a Tommy gun whom I could summon to Princeton from his Camden neighborhood in two seconds flat if need be.

So then Tiger said that I should probably learn the Wooden Dummy first, since it is a stationary opponent that doesn't hit back (I'm pretty sure it did hit me back). The Wooden Dummy is a solid wood contraption that looks to me like a wooden robot. It's supposed to represent a human sized opponent, with a vertical trunk about nine or ten inches in diameter, three short limbs about the size and length of forearms that represent the opponent's arms, two of them at shoulder height and one at stomach height (for a punch to the stomach?), and one long bent limb just above knee height that represents the opponent throwing a kick at you. Tiger worked through a dozen or more sets, each having a dozen or more individual moves that represented various ways that you would block and counter an opponent's attacks. I could memorize the moves and their names easy enough–Han Sau, Tan Sau, Bong Sau, Huen Sau, etc., but I just couldn't do them, because doing them involved slamming your forearm into the solid wooden limbs. After my forearm turned black, blue, red, purple, yellow, and green from my first try and felt even worse than it looked, Tiger relented. He explained that while he hit it hard to toughen his limbs for sparring in tournaments, hitting it hard was not necessary to become adept at Kung Fu.

"Come on, Joey," he said, "I learned this from my Lăolao."

"Your what?"

"My grandmother."

"Look," I said, "don't take this personally, but I would hate to meet your Lǎolao in a dark alley somewhere. She must be very frightening."

"Oh, if you saw her now you *would* be very frightened, because she's a ghost," he said. "But when she was alive she was a beautiful woman."

"She must have been a very strong woman is all I meant, if she taught you how to use this contraption."

"Ah yes, she was very strong, but not very tall and didn't look strong. She always said, 'One who excels as a warrior does not try to appear formidable.' My style of Kung Fu was created by a woman, a Buddhist nun, in the 1700's."

The Erhu Episode
– A Divertissement

(Advanced recombinant literary engineers will recognize a Divertissement as a shorter version of a full Divertimento. I may have these backwards; I shouldn't have to remind you that I'm a very mixed-up person.)

I SHOULD PAUSE FOR JUST A FEW SECONDS TO SHARE what I learned about Tiger's family, partly during our many conversations in college, and partly from a trunk of papers still in Tiger's possession, that I open occasionally to stimulate Tiger's memory, and which includes some beautiful paintings and drawings by his mother. Tiger's mother, Kuang Li Fang, was from a wealthy Chinese family that had fled to Hong Kong before the 1937 Japanese occupation of China, and later to England, when Japan attacked Hong Kong in December of 1941. Li Fang was 13 when they fled to England. Her older brother, Tiger's uncle, lost his life trying to aid the unsuccessful British military effort to save Hong Kong from the Japanese.

As an aside I should confess that I was very confused the first time Tiger tried to explain how in Chinese they put the surname first. "So in English, is your middle name Yu or Chin?"

"We don't have middle names; Yu Chin is my first name."

"Why do you call it first if you put it last?"

"That's a western term. We don't have it in China. Just call me Yu Chin."

"Why don't you leave my chin out of it?"

Now where was I? While in England, Li Fang and her parents, Tiger's maternal grandparents, stayed as guests of a wealthy British jade collector who was instrumental in helping them to flee Hong Kong. From time to time they were housed in his London flat, but mainly in his country cottage near Oxford. Oxford was deemed safer than London due to German bombing, greatly diminished since the blitz from September of 1940 to May of 1941, before they arrived, but still a threat throughout the war. Li Fang was enrolled in secondary school at Rye St. Antony in Headington, on the outskirts of Oxford. Since age seven, both in China and in Hong Kong, she had received instruction in traditional Chinese painting and calligraphy. Her parents were unable to find any instruction for Li Fang while in England. But they were able to get her the needed supplies from a merchant in London, so that she could at least continue to practice what she had already learned.

Each year her parents would present their host with a gift of jade that her father had carved. The first year they presented it during Chinese New Year. But for the next three years they decided to follow the western custom and present it at Christmas. They returned to Hong Kong after the war ended, and Li Fang was enrolled in St Paul's College for Girls, where she was able to continue her study of calligraphy and painting.

Li Fang's father, Kuang Jié, and his family had been in the jade carving and trading business for generations, and he had amassed a small fortune. They were from the city of Guangzhou (formerly Canton) in the Guangdong province, not far from Hong Kong. Kuang Jié met Tiger's maternal grandmother, Jiang Xiuling (Lǎolao), while on a trading trip to Hong Kong, where she was born. He did not learn that she was a Kung Fu expert until sometime after they were married, when she apparently had quite a surprise for a would-be robber. But he did learn right away that she was an expert at playing the Erhu.

The Erhu, a four-stringed instrument played with a bow, is the Chinese answer to the violin. It has a unique and very enchanting sound. Tiger introduced it to Mary and me during college with recordings he made of his grandmother playing. A friend of Tiger's convinced someone to play the Erhu at our wedding. The musician was the wife of a visiting professor from Taiwan. I'd like to think that our wedding guests with tears in their eyes missed Mary terribly, but it's just as likely that they were moved to tears by the enchanting, ethereal sound of the Erhu. Regardless of the source, Mary's roommate, who officiated at the wedding, said that tears are a river to God or something to that effect. I was in no mood to hear about God on that day. From the car accident, my dream girl was dead, my roommate had brain damage that left him unable to talk and temporarily confined to a wheelchair, and I had my broken jaw wired shut for the next six weeks, as well as three chipped vertebrae. I bawled the whole time; Tiger fell asleep and snored.

Lǎolao's parents (Tiger's maternal great-grandparents) had substantial real estate holdings in Shanghai and Hong Kong, and it was expected that a girl of her stature would get extensive training from early youth in some art form. The Kung Fu was not an art form in that sense, but her father, Jiang Min—Tiger's maternal great-grandfather—had one of his tenants, a Buddhist nun from the Henan province assigned to a hospital in Shanghai, train her for self-defense. Jiang Xiuling had extraordinary beauty, and when she was still a young child, a fortune teller advised her father that his beautiful daughter's eventual marriage would greatly enlarge his wealth, but only if he took great care to protect her from unworthy suitors.

Lucky for Tiger's grandfather, when he saw Jiang Xiuling playing the Erhu for her father's guests, he attempted, through some superhuman effort, to conceal from her father how gobsmacked he was by her astonishing beauty. Preceded by only the very slightest nod in her direction (a slight nod might suggest that he was enamored of her music, whereas a pronounced nod would suggest that he was enamored of her looks), he then faced her father and took the deepest, deepest bow he could muster. Then he whispered something to his two younger brothers sitting behind him, and from the big trunk they had on the floor between them, they took out a large leather pouch that contained the most beautiful jade carving he'd done in his entire life.

Kuang Jié, with his teenage brothers--the security team-- in tow, was in Hong Kong at the behest of Jiang Xiuling's father, who wanted to trade silver for some jade carvings. At that time in China both jade and silver were greatly valued as relatively safe and stable assets. Now where was I? So he handed the pouch to her father and said that it was an advance token of his appreciation, because he was of age to marry, and he hoped Jiang Min might mention Kuang Jié's name should Jiang Min happen to know of anyone with an eligible daughter who had even a *fraction* of Jiang Xiuling's talent and charm. He could not say talent and beauty; that would be too bold. But he could say talent and charm. Tiger said that it was a time of great instability in China, and the tradition of arranged marriages was breaking down, especially when families were scattered in different parts of China, Hong Kong, Macau and elsewhere, so his grandfather had to take matters into his own hands that were normally left to a matchmaker.

When recounting this story in our dorm room, on more than one occasion, Tiger would pace about the room with his chest out and gesticulating with great drama, "Lăolao's father—my great-grandfather—took one look inside the pouch and knew that *that* was no token of appreciation; that was a marriage proposal." It was a very intricate and exquisite carving, of two peacocks frolicking under a plum blossom tree, more like a piece of jewelry than of carved stone, but about the size of a football. The delicate scrollwork and play of light and shadow on the highly polished surfaces were more beautiful than anything that Lăolao's father had ever seen.

Jiang Min insisted on paying for it, but Kuang Jié insisted more strongly that it was a gift. (A Chinese custom still in practice is to refuse a gift two or three times, before finally accepting it.) So Lăolao's father, not to be outdone in generous overtures, bought Kuang Jié's entire trunk of jade carvings. Tiger said Lăolao told him that her father may have intended to buy the entire trunk of jade anyway, but it was absolutely out of character for him to buy it without negotiating the price. Needless to say, because Tiger would not have told me if the deed were not done, after extensive arrangements, intensive negotiations and so forth, they were married, their family fortunes were merged and eventually smuggled out of China into Hong Kong, and then before WWII into a Swiss bank account, while Tiger's maternal grandparents and his mother escaped to England.

Tiger's father, Yeung Wei, was born and raised in Hong Kong. Like two generations before him, he was destined to become a botanist. When Yeung Wei turned eighteen, Tiger's paternal grandfather sent him to study botany in the Yunnan province of China at the Kunming Institute of Botany, under the tutelage of an old college friend, in September of 1941, shortly before Japan attacked Hong Kong. Tiger's paternal grandparents lost their lives in Hong Kong during the war. But his father was safe in Yunnan, which remained out of reach of the Japanese invasion. He returned to Hong Kong in 1947 to help rebuild the Hong Kong Botanical Garden, which had been ravaged by the war. That's where he met and fell in love with Tiger's mother, who Tiger said was as beautiful as Lǎolao was at her age.

In Yunnan Tiger's father was safe from the war, but not from snakes. While out gathering plant specimens for his dissertation, he was bitten on the leg by a tree viper. His right leg was amputated below the knee. He wore a prosthesis that enabled him to amble about. Tiger's father was having second thoughts about his career choice, though, because his understandable fear of snakes, which he expected to dissipate over time, had only worsened.

I hope all this circling around isn't making anyone dizzy, but now we are back to Tiger's mother, Jiang Li Fang, in the spring of 1948, accompanied by her parents to an open house that the Hong Kong Botanical Garden was holding to stimulate interest and enlist volunteers to help in its restoration. This was an affair for the whole family, as it was one of their favorite places for a family stroll before the war.

She was there as a volunteer to help with flower planting. She also wanted to see how the restoration work was proceeding, and she hoped to scout out some subject matter for future paintings. Lǎolao, accompanied by other musicians, was to play a short Erhu recital.

Li Fang's father developed a lung disorder after many years of exposure to jade dust. Over the years, as his condition worsened, he had become an astute real estate investor and developer, under the tutelage of his father-in-law. And now he was poised to take part in the Hong Kong construction boom that resulted from the massive influx of refugees from China, where civil war had broken out again between the Nationalists and the Communists. But at heart a carver, and almost as good with wood as he was with jade, he volunteered to help restore some of the ancient wood carvings that had adorned the botanical garden's buildings before the war.

As fate would have it, on that spring day in 1948, Tiger's father was giving a talk about the flora that were lost in the war and about the plans to restore the gardens. It was obvious to Tiger's father from the start that Tiger's mother was rather attractive; he would say later that his wife was mistaken for Audrey Hepburn on more than one occasion. Yeung Wei was very self-conscious about his artificial leg and thought it made him the Hong Kong equivalent of *The Hunchback of Notre-Dame*. Li Fang, on the other hand, found it endearing. And more importantly, as time went on, so did her parents, especially since, due to his shyness, he was the perfect gentleman. There was another consideration as well, and he was painfully aware of it. Her family had great wealth, and he was a pauper, an orphan in fact. While he studied for his Ph.D., his parents stayed behind in Hong Kong and lost their lives and everything they owned. Now he was a newly minted Ph.D. and about to turn twenty-five, but nevertheless a pauper.

Li Fang's father saw this as a possible silver lining. He lost his only son in the war. In order to continue the family name, the Chinese had a custom called a *ruzhui* marriage, where a husband of lesser means moves in with the wife's family and the children take the mother's surname instead of the father's. Yeung Wei would have cut off his other leg on the spot for the chance to marry Li Fang, so anything short of that was fine with him. But it was Li Fang who argued with her father against the *ruzhui* marriage. "He lost his whole family," she said to her father, "and now you want to take his family name from him too?" Lǎolao had a soft spot for Yeung Wei as well. Hobbling around on his artificial leg, combined with his shyness and gentlemanly demeanor—always quoting Confucius, in her eyes he was quite the sympathetic character.

Eventually Kuang Jié saw the *ruzhui* marriage idea as a lost cause. By this time Li Fang knew all about her future husband's fear of snakes, and she played matchmaker between her father's need for a smart and trustworthy protégé in his burgeoning construction and development business and her soon-to-be husband's need for an alternative career.

The High-Rise Episode

SPIRALING INWARD OR OUTWARD, AS THE CASE MAY BE, back to our time at Princeton, it may be obvious why Tiger wanted to be an architect. Freud would say that he was seeking his father's approval, that Tiger wanted to design buildings for his father to build, all because of a "father complex." Herzog coined a phrase in 1980, "father hunger." But the Chinese have a tradition that started long before Freud, called Xiao or "filial piety," meaning to respect or honor your parents and ancestors, so that Tiger would not just seek his father's approval, but obey his father's wishes.

Tiger's father, who himself started out in his father's-- Tiger's paternal grandfather's--footsteps as a botanist, would not insist that Tiger study architecture. But as a toddler Tiger got to use his father's old blueprints for coloring, and as a teen he developed a keen interest in architecture. Tiger's father—I called him Mr. Yeung— was a builder/developer, not an architect. But having an architect in the family would have obvious advantages.

At the start of every fall semester, Mr. Yeung would fly

over from Hong Kong with Tiger to help get him settled. Starting in our sophomore year, he would invite me along when they went out to dinner at the French restaurant, Lahiere's, Princeton's most expensive restaurant at the time. It struck me as quite different from any restaurant I saw while growing up in a blue collar family. But I did love the lamb chops. I had them once or twice at my Nonna's house, but never at home, because my Nonno (grandfather) brought a baby lamb home to raise for food when my father was a child and my father thought of it as a pet. So he would never eat lamb after his "pet" was served for dinner.

In the beginning of our junior year, while eating at the French restaurant we were talking about architecture. Mr. Yeung wondered aloud how soon Tiger could design something for him. "Yu Xun, you can design for me a tall building for a small property? When can you do this?"

Tiger's nickname from his parents includes his given name combined with something the parents see in him. In this case Xun (pronounced "shewn") means very fast or swift, because even before Tiger could walk, he was always darting about, often too quickly for them to restrain him.

"Like a tall house, Bàba (Daddy in Chinese)? That I can do."

"No, Yu Xun, like a high-rise, many stories, but on small lot like a house lot. We have many small lots in all three cities (by this time they had expanded to Singapore and Taipei), too valuable for one house. Maybe one house wide, but forty or fifty houses tall would be good."

"Bàba, it will be many years before I can do that." This answer made his father frown. The rest of the dinner was eaten mostly in silence. But his father suggested to Tiger that he could now honor his deceased grandfather with a beautiful new home.

After we walked Mr. Yeung to the Nassau Inn, where he would spend the night before catching the train to New York in the morning, for his flight to Hong Kong, we were heading across campus back to our dorm. "What was your father saying about a new home for your grandfather? Isn't he dead?"

"Yes, he's dead. My mother's father is still alive, but not my father's father. Bàba's parents died when Japan attacked Hong Kong in 1941. We honor our ancestors on the anniversary of their death. We don't know the exact day my grandparents died, but we honor them on December 8th, the first day of the attack. We know a bomb hit their home, but we don't know what day it hit, because Hong Kong was in chaos then, until the British surrendered to Japan on December 25th."

"Wow, Tiger, you know your history."

"No, not history, my grandparents, not history. We honor them by learning about their lives."

"So are you going to build them a new home in Hong Kong?"

"No, you are crazy, Joey. We send them presents in the afterlife, by burning something we think they might want, like food, or money, or photographs. If I think they would like a beautiful new home, one that I could design, I could make it out of paper or cardboard. Then I would set it on fire as an offering to them."

"Well, that sounds a little crazy to me. Catholics just light candles for them at church."

"It's still fire, Joey. It sounds like you Catholics just borrowed our custom and made it easier on yourselves."

"Wait, don't blame me. I haven't set foot in a church since my confirmation at thirteen. In my family, the men don't have to go to church after they make confirmation."

"What? Then why do they call it confirmation? Sounds more like a *bon voyage* party to me, 'goodbye, nice knowing you.' If I were the Catholic church, I would just stop having confirmations. Then what would you do?"

"Oh, the men still go on holidays, mainly Christmas and Easter. And maybe Ash Wednesday. My dad is superstitious. He goes whenever he wants to ask God for a favor. I stopped going to church in my senior year of high school, when I read some books that really made my religion seem kind of silly. Did you ever read Bertrand Russell's *Why I Am Not a Christian?*"

"You read too many books, Joey, especially for someone without a brain. Oh, I forgot. You're a Rube Goldberg Machine. The words go in through your eyes. Then a sliding board takes them straight to your stomach, where they are absorbed, digested, and regurgitated, so that they come out of your mouth as baloney."

That fall Tiger commandeered the coffee table in our dorm room and built an elaborate mansion out of construction paper for his paternal grandparents. After dinner one night, I went with him down to Lake Carnegie at the bottom of the campus to watch him set it on a little homemade raft and light it on fire. It was on December 8th; I remember it was a Wednesday.

While he made no promises to his father, Tiger devoted a lot of his studies to what he called Bàba's "skinny high-rise" problem.

Princeton required all juniors and seniors to complete an independent study project, done under the tutelage and consent of a faculty advisor. It was a long written work--a thesis--for most students, and generally the senior thesis would have greater heft and more substance than the junior thesis. For some subjects, such as science, it may involve an experiment. In the arts it may involve a work of art, such as a sculpture, or a musical composition. In architecture it may involve a building design. A math major might try to solve some great mathematical conundrum.

Often the junior thesis will be a prelude, or prolegomena to the senior thesis. In Tiger's case, his junior thesis was a scholarly review of high-rise structural designs, such as concrete, steel and combinations of the two. And then his senior thesis was an actual design project—complete with blueprints, where he would design a high-rise, specifically a skinny high-rise.

Tiger liked to drink strong green tea and stay up all hours of the night studying until his teeth started chattering. I found it somewhat amusing that around campus he looked like one of the tough guys in a Bruce Lee movie, but at night in our dorm, he worked in pajamas that had Bonsai trees on them in our junior year and dragons in our senior year. Like most students, I had graduated by then from pajamas to gym clothes for sleeping attire.

Once during our senior year I got up the courage to tease him about it, "Tiger, are the dragon pajamas the Chinese version of our Donald Duck pajamas?"

"Ahh, that's very funny, Joey," accompanied with a hearty pat on the back that knocked the wind out of me.

Tiger's design for a skinny high-rise could not meet his father's needs for the smaller lots that would normally fit one house. But he thought he could do it on the lots that were big enough for two houses. The trouble with a skinny high-rise building is that it needs a minimal amount of space for what he termed the "core area," which would have at least one elevator, one stairwell, a trash room with trash chute, and room to move water, wastewater, and other utilities to and from the upper floors, whether for just one apartment or several per floor.

Added to the minimum core area requirement are structural requirements, such as some of the walls have to be "shear" walls, which prevent the building from crumbling like a house of cards. And the structural walls of each floor have to support the weight of all the floors above them. So whether the structure is steel, or concrete, or more commonly a combination of the two, the structural walls generally have to be thicker at the lower floors. Tiger considered a carbon fiber structure to save space, since it had already been used for fishing poles, auto parts and airplane parts for a number of years by then. One of his sketches has the floors resting on a carbon fiber mast, like a series of crow's nests on a sailing vessel. But he abandoned the idea when he found out how expensive it was, besides never being tried as a construction material before (it is used nowadays, *Popular Mechanics*, Jan. 21, 2010).

And then the whole edifice has to rest on concrete pilings or caissons, which are dug, drilled, or hammered into the ground, while the builder is very careful not to disturb the neighbors' building foundations in the process. So while your lot may be eighty feet wide, you may be able to build something only sixty feet wide, even if the zoning allowed a building seventy feet wide.

Compounding the core area and structural requirements is the Hong Kong Building Ordinance, first established in 1856, with a couple of major changes (1935, 1955) and innumerable minor changes over the years, all of which served to make it more strict, especially regarding stepping back the upper floors so that the neighbors and the street below are not kept in perpetual shade. This is hard to do if there are only a couple or a few units per floor.

Tiger designed the core walls to serve double duty as the shear walls, a widely used economical solution. But shear walls and core walls both have to be fire resistant, and shear walls have to be extra rigid, making the core area a considerable expense that has to be added to each floor. The more apartments that can share the cost of the core area, the better.

Nowadays they have the technology to build skinny high-rises, nicknamed "pencil towers," all over the world, but they were pretty rare back in the 1970's. Whenever I read something about them I share it with Tiger and it usually elicits a smile.

Tiger's senior project was for a twenty-to-forty-story residential building, with a ground floor that measured sixty by ninety feet. It would probably need a lot size at least eighty by one hundred and ten feet. Structurally his design could go forty stories. But the height would be limited by the zoning requirements for how much the upper floors had to be stepped back.

In a conversation I had with Tiger's father a year or so after college, he lamented that Tiger had not been able to design a high-rise that was both taller and skinnier. I admit that I may have exaggerated when I told him that before the accident Tiger had been working on a carbon fiber building that could go many more stories on an even smaller lot. A short while after this conversation I had a dream that convinced me I needed to confess to Tiger's father that I may have exaggerated.

Against my better judgement jc insists that I tell you about the dream. I told jc over and over again, "No more asides, digressions, divertimentos, or divertissements. I'm sticking to the story." All right, just this once, I suppose I could insert a brief Intermezzo, out of compassion for some of my novice colt readers, who may be trying to finish the book all in one sitting, in spite of my earlier warning that it should be entered slowly, like a refreshing but ice cold spring. In a way, I suppose jc is right. After all, this is a work of recombinant literary engineering.

The Operating Room
– An Intermezzo

Joseph Colocento, the famous physician,
Had just received an emergency admission.
The patient, Mary Malin, was a beautiful woman,
Whose brain was severed at the corpus callosum.

The carbon fiber high-rise that swayed in the clouds
Finally swayed so far that it bent to the ground.
It bent like a giant fishing rod, everyone said,
And a piece of glass hit the poor woman's head.

The Doctor did everything to keep her alive.
The patient needed a miracle to survive.
Experimental surgery had to be tried.
If not, this woman would surely have died.

He called a friend at the Star Wars Defense Command,
And asked if he might have a spare laser at hand.
His friend replied that he certainly could spare one,
Its computer, though, was locked in the pentagon.

Next he called his Nonno in Camden, New Jersey,
And asked for his help in doing the surgery.
His grandfather replied, "What's-a matter for you?
You think I have-a nothing-a better to do?"

The laser would fuse all the nerves that were busted,
But a computer's aim could not be trusted.
A man skilled at sticking toothpicks in a brasciole
Should aim the laser to make the severed brain whole.

The operation seemed to go very well.
His grandfather worked faster than . . . pell-mell?
But something went unexpectedly wrong.
When he was done, the left and right brain were one.

The corpus callosum nerve bundle joins the two,
But it also serves to separate them too.
Without the hemispheres' normal separation,
What would happen to their specialization?

In freaks of nature, the Doctor was told of old,
There are spiritual gifts untold to behold.
While watching for signs out of the ordinary,
What he observed was very extraordinary.

She went in patients' rooms, touching them with her hand,
And as soon as she touched them, they all would stand.
But the most bizarre thing the Doctor descried
Was when she awakened all the patients who died.

When back in her room, she spoke to him at last,
Saying something within reached a critical mass,
That inside everyone there is a divine light,

A little in the left brain, but most in the right.

That just below the surface we're not a pretty sight,
But deep within a candle burns so bright.
Everything she said, he hurried to write down,
Racing against time, and the alarm clock sound.

(ADVANCED STUDENTS OF RECOMBINANT LITERARY engineering will not recognize this. It is merely a cheap trick that I've employed since elementary school. When I can't remember what happened next, I simply have an alarm clock wake me from the dream.)

A Few Words About
Mary – An Entr'acte

The philosophy of six thousand years has not searched the
chambers and magazines of the soul. Man is a stream
whose source is hidden. Our being is descending into us
from we know not whence.

— Ralph Waldo Emerson ("The Over-
Soul")

As I said earlier, Mary and I met on a windy
afternoon in March of our junior year. We were both
exiting Firestone Library at the same time, and she kindly
held the door for me. I'm generally the chivalrous one. But I
was carrying a stack of books about a foot high, and she had
a light load. To be perfectly honest, I never had the
opportunity before that to be the chivalrous one. But I
always imagined that I would be chivalrous, should the
chance arise.

I hope it's not rude to interrupt myself. But very briefly
I want to take a minute to assure you that we are getting to
the main part of this book, namely the prairie, the

subconscious, and the soul, very shortly. I just feel that it would be self-centered of me to write about our time at Princeton without saying a few words about Mary.

I may have mentioned earlier that her eyes were radiant, which gave her a look of, on the one hand, maybe a Catholic Saint or an enlightened Zen Master, but on the other hand, possibly a madwoman. Her eyes were bright greenish blue, almost like jewels. "Your eyes are very sparkly," I said, "even under that beret of yours." I thought it looked like an oversized beret an artist wore. It had wide grey and blue stripes that were kind of faded.

"This was my grandfather's hat," she said, not telling me yet that he was forced to wear it while in the WWII concentration camps. "I'm trying to decide where I should go to have a cup of tea. Would you like to come along?"

"Er, how about Campus Club. We're the first club on Prospect Avenue. I'm on my way there." I hoped that I didn't sound as nervous as I felt.

"I'll take you up on that. I eat at Stevenson (a kosher alternative to the eating clubs), a bit further down Prospect. But it's not a club and there's no place to just hang out. Why don't I carry some of those books?"

"Er, no, that wouldn't work." Now I was fidgeting because I was afraid I forgot her name. "Sorry, I'm just very preoccupied. What was your name again?"

"I'm Mary. We haven't introduced ourselves yet. And you are?"

"Oh, that's great. So I didn't forget your name. I was so afraid that I might have forgotten your name already. I'm very forgetful, or absent-minded. I guess I'm both."

"And yours?" she reminded me.

"Oh, I'm Joe. So happy to meet you, Mary."

"Hi, Joe. Here, let me take a few of those books."

"Er, I couldn't let you do that," I turned to the side.

"Joe, this is 1977. Are you that old fashioned?"

"Yes. No. I don't know. I guess not. All right, take a few, but just a few." This wasn't done where I grew up. I agreed for the most part with the burgeoning feminist movement. But "the boy carrying the girl's books" was just so ingrained in me from my youth that it felt uncomfortable to switch roles. I'm not saying that any girl actually let me carry her books in my youth, just that it was the way things were done.

Campus Club was just a couple of blocks down Washington Road from the library, on the corner of Prospect Avenue. We were walking against the wind, and the top book blew off my pile. I stooped down to pick it up and dropped the whole pile. Now I was really making a fool of myself. "I meant to bring my gym bag with me to the library; I can carry a lot of books in it. But I forgot it. I'm an idiot. Are you sure you want to have tea with an idiot?"

"What are you working on, Joe?" she said as she helped me gather the books that were strewn on the sidewalk. "Ooh, *Man and his Symbols*," as she picked it up off the ground, "Carl Jung, I need to read that."

"It's for my junior thesis and it's crunch time. It's due next month."

"I thought they were due in the first week of May," she said. "I'm a junior too."

"My thesis advisor has an overloaded calendar in May, and I agreed to get it in early. I thought it would be good in the long run. I could concentrate on studying for final exams, without having to fret over my thesis."

"That's good thinking, Joe. Maybe you're not an idiot."

"Maybe the jury's still out on that."

Our conversation continued as we walked along the

tree-lined street. This time of year the trees, mostly Oak, Sycamore, Maple, and Elm, were still pretty bare. And with the blustery wind, it felt more like winter than the dawning of spring.

"Where are you from, Mary?"

"Me? Oh, Cedar Mills. Have you heard of it?"

"Ahh, you're from North Jersey. I'm from South Jersey, whole different planet. You're a suburb of New York and we're a suburb of Philly. I was born and raised in Camden, but my parents live in Bridgeview now."

"I heard of Camden. Where is Bridgeview?"

"Bridgeview is a small blue collar town along the Delaware, not too far north of Camden. It's about forty miles south of here."

"I don't know much about Camden, just that it has a Rutgers campus and that it's across from Philadelphia. But I know you South Jersey types. You go to Atlantic City, Cape May, and Wildwood; we go to Long Branch, Point Pleasant, and Asbury Park."

"Right, we get tanner because we're closer to the sun."

"You're about a hundred miles closer to the equator, but only a tiny, tiny, infinitesimal fraction of an inch closer to the sun. Still, too much sun is not healthy, Joe."

"Maybe not for a redhead, but I don't sunburn. Well, not as much."

"What's your major, Joe?"

"Psychology, isn't that what all crazy people study? I should say theoretical psychology, because people hear psychology, they think I'm trying to analyze them. That's clinical psych, very different. What's your major?"

"Religion and philosophy."

I was so mesmerized by her that I barely noticed that we had arrived and were in the front hall at Campus Club. I didn't remember opening the front door or setting my books down on the table inside the door. "Oh, here we are already. Follow me and we'll get some tea," I said, as we found our way into the butler's pantry, where several large coffee makers were kept hot all day, one of which was strictly for tea water. "What would you like? Let's see. We have Tetley, Lipton, and, er, Twinings Constant Comment. Oh, and here's a Twinings Earl Grey."

"I'll have the Constant Comment."

I had the coffee, which always tasted a little burnt by this time of day. Then we tried sitting on the second floor back terrace, but it was too windy. So we found a comfortable little table by a sunny window in the downstairs sunroom.

When we came in from the wind, I instinctively reached for my comb. She stopped me, saying, "Put that comb away. Chaos theory says that if you just leave your hair alone, eventually it will reorganize itself on a higher level."

"If you say so, I won't comb it. Do you want me to stand out on the terrace and spin around in the wind until it looks just right? Is that what you mean, that my hair will comb itself? Or will I look like a scarecrow? Does your hair comb itself?"

She chuckled. "Mine's short and curly," she said as she lifted her beret to show me. Then she gave me an introductory lesson on chaos theory, and how she was applying it, as best as she could anyway, to the marginalia in the Talmud. And she added that next year, for her senior thesis she would apply chaos theory to understanding the nature of God.

"I never heard of chaos theory. It sounds fascinating. But can it be applied to something that might not exist?

What if God doesn't exist? I'm Catholic, but I don't think I really believe in God anymore."

"That's next year. This year I'm just trying to straighten up the Talmud a little. It needs a woman's touch."

"Wait, I thought you said it's 1977. Why a woman's touch? Are you old fashioned too?"

"Why a woman's touch? Why not? That's exactly why. Women are better at a lot of things than men. I happen to be a very 'organized thinker,' to quote my thesis advisor, Professor Kaufmann."

"I never heard of him; is he in religion or philosophy?"

"Philosophy. Did you ever read his *Critique*?"

"Critique of what? I never heard of it."

"His *Critique of Religion and Philosophy*. He's brilliant. He's one of the foremost Nietzsche scholars in the world."

"No, I haven't heard of Kaufmann." I would learn about Professor Kaufmann before the junior year was over, after Mary would learn that I'm a carpenter, and after Professor Kaufmann would mention that he needed a carpenter for some repairs around his house.

The Talmud Episode

It may be said that it is a book containing laws and discussions, philosophic, theologic, and juridic dicta, historical notes and national reminiscences, injunctions and prohibitions controlling all the positions and relations of life, curious, quaint tales, ideal maxims and proverbs, uplifting legends, charming lyrical outbursts [my personal favorite], and attractive enigmas side by side with misanthropic utterances, bewildering medical prescriptions, superstitious practices, expressions of deep agony, peculiar astrological charms, and rambling digressions on law, zoology, and botany, and when all this has been said, not half its contents have been told.

— Gustave Karpeles

I SHOULDN'T CALL THIS AN EPISODE, SINCE IT'S ABOUT Mary, and she doesn't have episodes. Mary has a very organized mind. Her mind is like the lawn I described earlier, mowed first from front to back in neat rows, then crisscrossed from side to side for extra measure, the hedges neatly trimmed, the sidewalk edged, and all the flower beds carefully weeded and mulched. Whereas my mind is organized like the path your lawnmower would make through your yard if it were hitched up to the tail of a bucking bronco. And according to the publisher's legal department, anything coming out of it should be called an *episode*.

I can't remember who said it; I think it was Saul Bellow. He said that looking within the mind is like using an usher's flashlight in a dark theater. That may describe my mind, except it's a dark and *abandoned* theater, because my mind seems to have vacated the premises long ago. Mary's mind is quite the opposite. It shines like a lighthouse beacon: first it shines a bright light—an astounding insight, a thoughtful answer, a diplomatic parsing of opposing views—at you, and then you could almost see it rotating inward, as it surveys the inner landscape (maybe the prairie), until it circles three hundred and sixty degrees to shine out again. Throughout all our conversations this happened with the regularity of a lighthouse beacon.

"What's *your* thesis about, Joe?"

"Hey, wait. Don't change the subject."

"Don't change what subject?" she said.

"God. Does your thesis fall apart if he doesn't exist?"

"I don't think so. I'm using chaos theory to define God, not to prove God exists. One can define a Unicorn without having to prove it exists. Philosophers since Kant have agreed that existence is not a predicate."

"But what if I say, 'God exists?' Isn't existence a predicate in that sentence?"

"Yes, in grammatical terms, everything in a sentence that's not the subject is the predicate. But Kant meant that existence is not a predicate in a stricter sense, where predicate is defined as an attribute of a thing's essence. Philosophy makes a distinction between existence and essence. Also, I'm not limiting it to my religion. I'm going to throw every religion's and even every non-religion's view into the mix, and see if there's an underlying picture, if you will, of God. I suspect that the different religions are like the proverbial blind men trying to describe an elephant by the part they touched. But I think chaos theory will help me see the whole picture in a way that hasn't been seen before."

"What if all the different views cancel each other out, like the Michelson-Morley double slit light wave experiment I saw in Physics 101?"

"I took Professor Wheeler's Physics for Poets, but that was Thomas Young, in 1801, not Michelson-Morley. Very funny, Joe, but I don't think it applies."

"I wanted to take Physics for Poets, but it was full, so I took Physics 101. Professor Wilkinson gave me a C on my final. He said I would have got an A if I was in your class."

(I still wonder, after all these years, if we were in the same class and met there, in our freshman year, would we have fallen in love then, and have had two more years together? Or what if I approached her when she was having a bad day, and she shrugged me off, would I go scurrying away with my head down, never to try again? Or would I be undeterred? I'm not saying that I would have had the courage to approach her in the first place; I'm just wondering aloud how it might have turned out if I did.)

"My class was probably easier."

"It wasn't that. We had an essay question on quantum mechanics. It just required a general definition, suitable for freshmen. The idea popped into my head that quantum mechanics makes perfect sense once you see that 'to be or not to be' isn't the question; it's the answer. I didn't say anything beyond that. I thought it was self-explanatory. He said I deserved an A for the insight, but an F for lack of argument to support it. So he gave me a C. He said it would have been an A answer from a poet, because poets, like oracles, do not have to explain their utterances."

"It should have been obvious to him that you must be a poet."

"I should have mentioned that to him. So what do you think about God?" I asked.

"You really want to know what I think?"

"Yes, of course. I am the farthest thing from a clear thinker. It would be nice to hear a clear thinker's take on it."

"After my freshman year I told Father that I was struggling with my belief in God."

"What did he say?"

"Shush! That's what he told me."

"He told you to shut up? My roommate would say that. It's very Zen."

"He said that I should go speak with the Rabbi at our synagogue in Cedar Mills."

"Did your Rabbi help you?"

"No."

"So you're like me; you don't believe."

"Joe, if you want to hear this, then you have to stop interrupting."

"Oh, I'm sorry. I get that complaint a lot here. Italians all talk in unison. You should see us at the kitchen table. Everyone listens and talks at the same time."

"I do believe. Our Rabbi thought I should speak with a woman at our synagogue. She was widowed at a young age and then went a little wild. Her husband was somewhat repressive and she felt like a bird let out of a cage when he died. She lost her faith, but eventually found it again."

"So you met with her?"

"Yes, and she told me that the inside of our mind is like a big house. Sometimes we run all over the house, from the basement to the attic, through every room on every floor, shouting, sometimes pleading, crying out, even in tears, 'God, where are you, where are you, God?' questioning, louder, 'GOD? Are you here? Dammit! There is no God,' until you come to a closet that's locked from the outside. God taps on the door from inside. 'It's me. I'm here. You yourself locked me in here, so I wouldn't see the mess you made of your house.' I felt that my situation was similar to this woman's. Not that I went wild. But the sudden freedom of not living at home made me question what I really wanted to do, and what I really believed."

"Did you find God locked in a closet in your mind?"

"Of course not in a literal sense, but yes, I could see that scenario playing out in my head to some degree. How about you? Did you lock him in a closet in your mind?"

"No. I stopped believing sometime in high school. But my aunts know a Jesuit priest, Father David, who they think has the power to heal others. They had him come and pray for my cousin, who had polio. She wasn't cured. But they didn't expect the priest to have a hundred percent cure rate. He comes to our family gatherings often, and he has a sense of humor. He was at my Nonna's Christmas Eve."

"Wait, I heard that word before. Is that your grandmother?"

"Yes, so he said, 'I had the flu with a fever recently, and my cat jumped on my bed and laid her paws on me. Was she laying on hands, trying to heal me? Or was she hoping I would die any minute, so she could munch on my fingers?' I learned from him that the Jesuit order was originally established to defend the Catholic faith, but that they had evolved to become the defenders of the downtrodden, especially in South America. I was so impressed with him that I thought about becoming a Jesuit. But I just couldn't. I'd have to lie and say that I believed in God."

"Did you ever read Nietzsche's *Genealogy of Morals*? That's a tough one to swallow and still have faith. I still do in spite of it. But I've learned to take all so-called canonical writings with a grain of salt. They have a glimpse of the truth about God, but not much more."

"I haven't read anything by Nietzsche. I could get around some of the arguments I've heard against believing, but I can't get around what I read in John Stuart Mill's autobiography. His father studied at Edinburgh to become a preacher, but never preached because he said that he couldn't believe in a God who was omniscient, omnipotent and benevolent, yet who created the human race—in his own image no less—with the 'infallible foreknowledge,' and therefore the *intent*, that most of us would be subject to eternal torture in hell, a hell that he himself created."

"I haven't read Mill's autobiography, Joe. But that's exactly what I'm talking about. The Talmud strongly cautions against taking the scriptures literally. We don't have a hell in Judaism like the Christian hell. We have the terms Sheol and Gehenna to represent places one's soul might go to pay for his sins after death, but they are closer in concept to the Christian purgatory than hell. And the time spent there is no longer than twelve months for all but the most evil. Some Jews believe that death is nothingness; one would simply cease to exist. Others believe that after you pay for your sins in Sheol or Gehenna, your soul rises to a heavenly place called Olam Habah, which is a lot like the Garden of Eden. Still others have a more mystical belief that after you pay for your sins, your soul begins an upward climb on a spiritual ladder that leads through all sorts of heavenly rungs, until you get closer and closer to the ineffable Ein Sof, God the unknowable. We have a saying, 'Two Jews, three opinions,' which is very apropos here."

Then she told me about a dispute in the Talmud (Eruvin 13b) between the schools of two sages, Hillel and Shammai, over the interpretation of certain *halakha* (*Jewish law*). A divine voice arose and said that both schools' interpretations could be correct, but that they should follow the Hillel school's interpretation, because they were "agreeable and forbearing, showing restraint when affronted, and when they taught the *halakha*, they would teach [both interpretations]."

"Well, that's a nice story, Mary. So the saying is true, that God—if there *is* a God—exalts the humble?"

"Yes, that's the main lesson of this story, but it also cautions against taking the scriptures literally. The Talmud's lessons are woven together, and intertwined, lessons on top of lessons, lessons within lessons, and between lessons. It's a virtual superfetation of wisdom."

"A super *what?*"

"Oh, sorry, that's a super abundance of something, like flower blossoms on a gladiolus. That's why the Talmud appears to be in chaos. Just in this little story, there's another obvious lesson. The heavenly voice said that the people in the school of Hillel were 'agreeable;' they were nice people. Listen. I'd better get to Stevenson; it's near dinner time."

"Can we continue this conversation sometime? Can I call you?"

"I was hoping you'd say that," she answered.

"Let me walk you to Stevenson."

"No, you don't have to."

"Yes, I do. I'm a little old fashioned."

The Phone Rehearsal Episode

The mind races around like a foraging squirrel in a park, grabbing in turn at a flashing phone-screen, a distant mark on the wall, a clink of cups, a cloud that resembles a whale, a memory of something a friend said yesterday, a twinge in a knee, a pressing deadline...a tick of the clock... Left to itself the mind reaches out in all directions as long as it is awake – and even carries on doing it in the dreaming phase of its sleep.

— Sarah Bakewell

MIDTERMS WERE UPON US, SO I DIDN'T CALL HER UNTIL the end of midterm week, about two weeks after we met. No, that's another bald-faced lie. I was scared to death to call her. She could see that I was clumsy, and she knew that I was a gentile—what's worse, a non-believing gentile. In addition to two strikes against me, I just reimagined our conversation in a way that I'm sure made her see that I was both a little nuts and an idiot to boot.

I only called her because Tiger was sick of seeing me

grab the phone and then put it down a couple dozen times in the last two weeks. So he threatened to call her on my behalf. That, I thought, would add a fifth strike against me, scared of girls. In hindsight, I would never have had the courage to ask for her phone number during our earlier conversation. Although I wasn't aware of him back then, jc must have blurted that out.

Tiger helped me craft my first line, and then rehearsed possible scenarios with me. "Say, 'Hello, Mary, I'm sorry I haven't called sooner, but I didn't want to bother you during mid-terms.' No, don't say bother. That's a very negative word. Just say that you felt you really had to crunch to get through mid-terms. And you've been waiting anxiously. No, don't use that word either. You've been waiting for your head to clear so you could plan something to do together. Your head will never clear, Joey. Just say you thought it best to call after midterms. Okay? Let's rehearse."

I must say, I'm a ridiculous man. She sounded very happy to hear from me. That made the next part easier than I thought it would be during rehearsals with Tiger. I asked her if she would like to come with me tonight to hang out at Campus Club. "It's a small celebration that they have after midterms. They usually have a band or a DJ, but probably not tonight. Some of the students already left for spring break."

"Joe, I'd like that. But I'm leaving for spring break tonight. I was just packing laundry to take home. Mother is picking me up. Tomorrow we're flying to visit my Aunt Edna in Saint Augustine, Florida for a few days. I can go to your club with you when I come back. How about Saturday after spring break? Joe, Joe, are you there?"

"Yeah, yes, sure, oh, that sounds great." I was in an epic battle with my urge to interrupt her with oh, I understand, you can't, well, no problem, maybe some other time, and so on, that I almost didn't hear her. Then I practically passed out when I realized what she said. "Saturday after spring break? Okay, sure. Can I walk you there? Should I meet you outside your dorm? Want to meet outside my dorm? Want to get a bite to eat first? I can take you to the Annex or Hoagie Haven. That's two Saturdays from tomorrow, right? I'd better write this down. There should be a band. I'll see if there's a band. But they'll at least have a DJ."

"Yes, two Saturdays from now. You could meet me at Stevenson. I'll probably have dinner there. But we could just meet at your club. What time does their party start?"

"Usually if it's a DJ, he'll start playing music around eight. If there's a band, they start tuning their instruments around the same time. I could meet you at Stevenson around seven-thirty. Is that good? Two Saturdays from now, right?"

"Yes. Two Saturdays. Seven-thirty. Stevenson. Aren't you going away for spring break?"

"I can't. Did I tell you I was a carpenter? I do small repairs for some of the clubs, and spring break is a good time to get one of the bigger projects done. The manager of my club is responsible for five or six of the other clubs, and there's always something that needs fixing—doors that won't close, wood rot, broken dumbwaiters, wall and ceiling repairs. I mean, there's a million things that need fixing. This week I'm rebuilding the front door for one of the clubs down the street. The bottom rail is coming loose from the stiles."

"I don't know what that is, Joe."

"Oh, I'm sorry. The bottom of the door needs to be taken apart and reassembled. It will take almost a week, if my idea for fixing it works. I have to take the door off the hinges and leave it on sawhorses for several days. So I have to put up some temporary plywood over the opening while the door is off. Do you want to hear more?"

"I'd like to hear more about how you learned carpentry. Some students come here with skills playing a musical instrument, or ballet, or sports; but carpentry?"

"I know, carpentry is not very intellectual. I come from a blue collar family and a blue collar town. Please don't think I'm someone I'm not. I would not be in Campus Club or any club if the manager didn't allow me to cover the extra dining expense with carpentry projects."

"Joe, I wasn't saying that at all. I'm actually very impressed. I've never even met a carpenter before. I mean there is so much to learn, isn't there? Where would you begin? How do you have time?"

"I'll tell you more after you get back if you like. My father taught me everything."

"Okay, Joe, see you then. I'll be back next Sunday night for classes next Monday. Maybe we could have tea one afternoon."

I called her on the Monday after spring break and had to hang up immediately. "Tiger, she has an answering machine. What do I say to an answering machine? Yikes."

Tiger helped me rehearse my line, "Hi, Mary, just calling to see if you'd like to have tea tomorrow or Wednesday afternoon. You can ring me back if interested."

"This is Mary."

"Oh, it is you. I thought it was your answering machine."

"I thought you were a robot."

"I was reading it. Sorry, I get tongue-tied with answering machines. How did you get one in a dorm room? Aren't they expensive?"

"It's my roommate's; her parents are pretty well off. Mother loves it. If I miss her call, I get her message and I can call her back. She offered to split the cost with my roommate's parents, but they said it would be too complicated, since they write it off as a business expense."

"So er, want to meet tomorrow or Wednesday for tea?"

"Sure. How about tomorrow at three. Want me to stop by your club? Or we could meet at the pub."

"The club sounds good. At that time of day it should be pretty quiet. You don't have to knock or anything. I'll be sitting in the living room, just off the entry hall."

I watched for her from a window in the living room. She wasn't wearing her beret. Instead, she had a big red shawl wrapped around her neck and draped over her shoulders. Princeton in March is often very chilly in the mornings and mild in the afternoons. So we dressed in layers. She probably had the shawl over her head and shoulders in the morning. I'm not one hundred percent sure about her outfit. After losing her so suddenly, I've tried to remember every single encounter and every single conversation we ever had. For almost all of our times together, it seems that I'm able to relive the whole conversation, just as though I was there again. But I can't honestly say that it's not being invented whole cloth by my subconscious. I was in a state that the psychologists call *limerence*—an infatuation so strong that if I didn't know better I'd swear that she had a gold aura. Or maybe it was a halo.

I remember, though, under the red shawl she had a light denim jacket, over a brown sweater, and dark brown corduroy bellbottoms. And she wore hi-top Moccasins. Since high school I have worn suede desert boots. Mary was fond of them, so I still wear them to this day. But she made me buy a pair of penny loafers for our wedding. I never really broke them in. When I tried to put them on about ten years ago for my father's funeral, they were too narrow. My doctor said that feet get flatter and wider as we age.

Where was I? Oh. After she got her tea, and I my coffee, we sat down on the living room couch. She wanted to know what my thesis was about.

"Is it about Carl Jung? When we met you said that stack of books was for your thesis."

"It's about why we dream."

"Oh, I've heard about that. All the symbolism. That's what that book was about, right?"

"Sort of, it was and it wasn't. My thesis is that dreams give us a rest from having to focus on things all day. It's called selective inhibition. When I look at you, I also see the wall behind you, the ceiling, the carpet on the floor, the lamp beside you, the end table, the coffee table, the mug, the stack of magazines, the window, the door to the TV room— and that's just the background. Looking at you, I see your red hair, your red shawl, your denim jacket, your sweater, your earrings—very pretty. Are they turquoise?"

"They are."

"Beautiful, they match your eyes. Do they? I don't know."

"They do, sort of, yes. So what were you saying about dreams?"

"Oh, focus. We don't focus during dreams. We remember seeming to focus after we wake up from the dream, but that's just our conscious mind trying to make sense of it. Actually the dream jumps all over the place. There are exceptions, but as they say, that just proves the rule. The rule is only a rule of thumb anyway. When I look at you, or at anyone for that matter, I tune out everything but what I am focused on. Like now it might be your eyes, or your lips—are you smiling, or frowning, or sad? I might make a mental note of that and then shift my focus to a blaring car horn out front. But even when my focus shifts, it's still focused on one thing at a time. So my brain is working ten times as hard to tune *out* ten other stimuli than it is to tune *in* one stimulus. And not just visual stimuli but sounds and smells as well."

"So what does all this have to do with Carl Jung and symbols?"

"Nothing really. But my thesis has to discuss all the other interpretations for why we dream, not necessarily to discount them. They could be operative on one level, while my theory—I'll call it that now—may be operative on another level at the same time."

"So what made you think of it, Joe?"

"I have no idea. It just sort of popped into my head while I was reading about dreams in Professor Jaynes' working draft of a book he's supposed to get published next year. It's about how consciousness originated."

"Who is he? Is he in the psychology department?"

"Oh, Julian Jaynes. He's my thesis advisor. He's using his manuscript in a class I'm taking on consciousness. I lucked out to get him. He's very busy putting final touches on his book. I met a grad student of his who taught a precept for his class last year. Every so often in the precept I would blurt out something. Sometimes he said it didn't make any sense, and other times he said it really hit the mark. He invited me to join the small group that meets at the Annex regularly, where Professor Jaynes holds court through the evening with his graduate and undergraduate advisees. But this is all beside the point."

"What point?"

"That during a precept on dreams, I blurted out that

they give our brains a rest from having to focus all day. I don't know about you, but for me it's very hard to focus. So it must be very tiring. How about you?"

"I don't know, Joe. I guess I always thought it was one of my strong points."

"But still, you see that while we are focusing on things, from the moment we wake up, until we drift off to sleep at night, we are simultaneously trying to ignore dozens of other things?"

"I never really thought about it, but sure, it makes sense."

"So we were reading Jaynes' discussion of dreams in his manuscript, and I blurted out my idea. Then Stevan—he's the grad student preceptor—said, 'Joe, that would make an interesting junior thesis topic.' I took the bait, and now I have to find as many justifications for it as I can. That's why I had that stack of books the day we met. I had to see what all the famous psychologists said about dreams. There are so many—William James, Sigmund Freud, Alfred Adler, Carl Jung, Erich Fromm, and B. F. Skinner are well known. But I had to research the lesser known ones as well. Ever hear of Havelock Ellis?"

"No, I can't say that I have."

"Well, he said, 'Dreams are real while they last. Can we, at best, say more of life?'" Mary liked that; she made me repeat it so she could write it down.

If I could briefly circle back, or spiral in, or maybe spiral out, to Saint Augustine—I assure you, this is part of the central discussion, not an aside or digression—and why I decided after graduation to move there. Mary said that Saint Augustine, where she had visited her Aunt Edna on numerous occasions, was her favorite place in the whole world. She loved the cobblestone streets and the old world charm of its many historical buildings. We had planned to eventually settle there after Mary finished grad school. After her death I felt her presence with me constantly, although nowhere as acutely as when I sat beside her grave. I thought that if I moved to Saint Augustine, then she would somehow get to accompany me. That still works after all these years. But I have found that visiting her grave gives me a much stronger sense of her presence than here in Saint Augustine. I still talk to her every day, like she's right here with me. But as I may have mentioned earlier, I take a lot of train rides to her grave as well.

The Nothing Dance Episode

AFTER WE FINISHED OUR TEA AND COFFEE, I WALKED her to her dorm at Holder Hall, which wasn't too far from my dorm at Lockhart Hall. "So I'll meet you at seven-thirty Saturday at Stevenson, right?"

"Yes. I'm looking forward to it, Joe. Should I wear my dancing shoes?"

"I should warn you I'm not a very good dancer."

Tiger wasn't there when I got back to our room. I just paced around, trying to absorb it all, fidgeting and talking to myself, until Tiger came in.

"What's up, Joey? You got your thesis ready? Is that why you're pacing? You have to shave that mustache, Joey."

"No, no and no. My Nonna said I have a long face, and a mustache makes it look not so long."

"Your Nonna is right, Joey. Your face looks shorter. But your mustache makes your nose look much longer. Before, you had a long nose. Now you have a giant nose. It looks like a two-story, Michaelangelo sculpture of a nose, sitting on a pedestal about the size and shape of a Chevy Impala."

"Well thank you, Tiger. Now I'm sure it's not a date. How can she date someone with a nose like that!"

"What date?"

"I don't know. Is it a date? Are we dating yet? I'm trying to remember everything she said, her body language, everything. I think it's a date."

"Oh, that girl Mary, right?"

"Yes, this is the second time we met for coffee. Well, she drinks tea. I'm taking her to our club party this Saturday."

"You told me that last week. So she's still going with you? That's good, Joey."

"You know more than me about girls, Tiger. Does that mean we're dating?"

"Joey, if you want my two cents, don't ever be the first one to say you're dating or in a relationship. Let her say it first. Then, if you like her, you agree with her."

"What? Are you sure about that? What if someone gave her the same advice, and then neither of us ever knows?"

"I just know, Joey, that most of the time the boy thinks he's in a relationship, and then finds out that he's the only one in it. Lǎolao told me that. The Tao says, 'Do you have the patience to wait until the mud settles and the water is clear?' My father told me that."

"I don't think I could be a Taoist, Tiger. I don't have any patience." I couldn't wait until Saturday, but I didn't have a choice. So, except for playing pool with Tiger every night after dinner for an hour or two, I buried myself in my studies as much as I could. Tiger and I started playing pool together regularly as freshmen. There are tables scattered all over campus in dorms, and of course at all the clubs. I learned to play pool at a bowling alley when I was thirteen.

We both joined Campus Club in the fall of our junior year. Most of the clubs were *selective*, and you had to *bicker* to get in, sort of like pledging a fraternity. But Campus and a few of the others had changed to membership by lottery. And like most of the clubs by this time, Campus was coed.

Finally, Saturday night arrived; Mary and I were walking along Prospect Avenue. I remember she was wearing a yellow and purple flowered dress. She wore it with her denim jacket and what I remember as combat boots. I would say she was going for the look of somewhere between a Haight-Ashbury flower child and a poor Jewish mountain girl from Appalachia. I was relieved that she wasn't going for the disco look, because I wasn't able to do the popular dances back then—the *bump* or the *hustle*, if my life depended on it.

"How did your door repair go? Did you finish it? Which club was it?"

"We just passed it. I think it was Cloister Inn. I got lucky on that. The joints needed to be reglued, but the wood was really solid. It was tricky, though. I had to make a new mortise and tenon joint on one corner. And I had to clamp it with a rope tied like a tourniquet, because the Gothic arched top wouldn't hold a regular clamp."

"I don't know what kind of joint that is, Joey. Mother likes antiques, and she looks for finger joints when she buys furniture."

"A mortise and tenon joint does something similar; it increases the surface area for the glue to hold."

"So if you had to make a new joint, then what made you feel lucky?"

"Well, I didn't expect the wood to be in such good shape. I guess it's because the door sits back in a deep recess, protected from the rain. But the main reason is that I gave the manager a bill for four hundred and thirty dollars for my time, and he handed me a check for a thousand dollars."

"Wow, Joey. Did he make a mistake?"

"I said, 'What's this for?' He said that he couldn't find anyone locally to fix it, that a company in Chicago would rebuild it for three thousand dollars and another company in Montreal would make a new door for six thousand. And both wanted several hundred each way for shipping. So he said I saved him a lot of money."

"That sounds like a lot of money for a door."

"Well, we don't notice them every day. But the club doors are very large, and most have intricate carvings. That door was two and a half inches thick, over four feet wide, and over eight feet tall. Besides the pointed Gothic arch, it had a lot of carvings. They don't make them like that anymore. I had to get Tiger to help me lift it. After getting paid so much, I offered him a hundred dollars for his help, but he wouldn't take it. He said his father gives him money when he needs it."

Now we had arrived at Campus Club. Tiger was coming down the stairs with an empty beer mug. "Hey, Joey, we have a serious pool game upstairs. One more beer and I'll be in the perfect shape to win. Who is this?" (As if he hadn't heard me say her name a hundred times already.)

"This is Mary. Mary, this is my roommate, Tiger. That's his nickname. His real name is Yu Chin. Just call him Tiger."

"Are you two coming down to the bar with me for a beer? Oh, no; that's right. Joey's a Dago Wine drinker. That should be your nickname, Joey: Dago Wino. Why don't you drink plum wine like a normal person? Does Mary know your real nickname? Mary, allow me to present to you," he said while taking a bow, "the Godfather of Lockhart Hall, otherwise known as the notorious kingpin, Joey Nostrils."

"Joey Nostrils? That's a cute name. Can I call you that, Joey?"

"Sure," I said. "But I'm not a kingpin."

"Yes he is, Mary. Don't come around him when he has a cold. When he sneezes he can blow you into the next town."

"He has a nose like my Father's. It's a Mediterranean nose. I like it."

"Joey, what's wrong with this girl? Mary, where's your glasses? Let me guess. Joey tripped and fell as he walked by you and accidentally knocked your glasses off, right? That's his standard operating procedure for meeting girls. So then he profusely apologizes and offers to buy you a coffee, right? Of course you can't see very well, so you say yes. Joey, you better stop pulling this stunt. She's just gonna break up with you when she gets her new glasses."

"Thank you, Tiger for such a kind introduction. I'm sure Mary believes every word you just said, especially since she doesn't wear glasses. I'll return the favor the next time I see *you* with a girl."

The bar was in the basement. It's called a walkout basement, just partly underground. I kept some of my family's red wine—Dago Red—in the downstairs refrigerator by the bar. "Mary, would you like a beer, or, er, would you like to try my Nonno's homemade red wine?"

"Your grandfather, right? I'd love to try some, Joe, oh I mean, Joey Nostrils. I like Chablis, but I'm curious about your wine. Tell me about it."

"Let's try a little first," as I poured some out into the twelve-ounce plastic glasses we had as the official Campus Club party glassware, regardless of what you were drinking.

"Oh, Joey, that's interesting. I don't know very much about red wines, except for an occasional glass of Manischewitz with meals. But Mother likes Chablis, and

I'll usually have that when it's in the house. What am I tasting, Joe? It's a little tart, and a little toasty; it's very nice."

"You're tasting the barest hint, no, I would say the faintest apparition of vinegar, and an oak barrel that's been on fire."

"Doesn't wine turn to vinegar if left out too long?"

"Yes. But this wine is made that way, not on purpose. Every year, Nonno and my father, several of my uncles, all of their friends, and all of their friends of friends, chip in and get a train-car load of Zinfandel grapes from California. They take home whatever their share is and make wine in big oak barrels, usually in their basements."

She took another sip, so I took another sip. "When I was young, Father would give me a glass of Seven-Up or Sprite with a little Manischewitz in it."

"Mine too, except as far back as I can remember, it was mostly wine with a little soda in it. I still like a splash of soda in it sometimes. It makes it less tart."

"I wouldn't mind a splash of soda in mine now, Joey."

"Okay, let me see if there's any behind the bar." I found an open bottle of Sprite and poured a small splash of it in her wine.

"Ooh, that's just right, Joe."

"Well, if you like that, I can pour you a little more and we can go upstairs and sit on the terrace." The weather was much milder that night than the last time we tried to sit out on the terrace. As we headed up from the basement, the band was tuning up in the dining room. As usual, the tables were stacked in the adjoining sunroom to make room for a dance floor.

Right at the top of the stairs, on the left, a pair of double French doors opened into the billiard room. We could see Tiger leaning over the table to make a shot. It looked like three or four guys were playing a serious game of Nine Ball. Most pool table games are played with fifteen balls, numbered one through fifteen. Nine Ball is played with the first nine balls, and they have to be sunk in order. You win if you sink the nine ball, even if your opponent sunk the first eight balls. It can be played by any number of people at once.

"Shh!" I said, "Tiger flips out if he thinks someone is trying to distract him."

"Oh, okay," she whispered, "I completely understand. We have a table at home and Father taught me to play."

We sat out on the terrace and talked for a while. It was getting a little chilly, so she buttoned up her denim jacket. "So, when they make the wine in the barrels, sometimes it turns to vinegar."

"So that's what I smell. But yes, it is very faint."

"That's because the barrels are expensive, and the only way to get rid of the vinegar smell is to burn it out. So they line the bottom with some gravel, to keep from burning a hole in it. And then they let a little fire burn in it, until the sides turn black from the heat and smoke. Then they scrape the sides. They repeat the same process a few times, until the vinegar smell is mostly gone. But the next batch of wine would have the faint hint of vinegar and a strong hint of toasted oak."

"Well, I do like it, Joe, especially with a splash of soda."

Then we talked about our childhoods. She told me about her dog Darwin, the backyard excavations, and the Ben Franklin incident, that I believe I mentioned earlier. And I told her how, in my childhood, my father would embarrass me in church.

"Joey, I found something that might help you with your dream thesis."

"Oh? I'm just sort of making it up as I go. But what did you find?"

"I'm reading Aldous Huxley's *The Doors of Perception*. He mentioned a philosopher—I think it was Henri Bergson--who had a theory similar to your idea of selective inhibition. He used a different term, but it sounded like the same thing. He said the brain was more eliminative than productive, that it acted like a reducing valve so you wouldn't get overwhelmed by too much information."

"I think I probably need to borrow that book, Mary."

"There are several copies in the library; let me know if you can't get one. You can borrow mine. It's pretty marked up, though."

The band started playing Santana's "Oye Como Va," and Mary's shoulders started bouncing up and down and doing hiccups, like she wanted to dance. Usually the clubs would hire bands from the New Brunswick area, who mostly played at Rutgers fraternities. But tonight we had a band from our school that was very popular and could play a wide variety of songs. Their conga player was especially good. He was my inspiration for trying to learn it. But like Tiger said, I did not dig a deep well and I did not hit water.

"Joey, let's go downstairs and dance a little. Did you grow up watching *American Bandstand* like I did? How about *Soul Train*, do you watch that?"

I knew this was coming. "Er, I had to work with my father most Saturdays. But I caught *Bandstand* once in a while, and some of *Soul Train*. I warned you I'm not a good dancer." I didn't tell her that I watched as much of *Soul Train* as I could in high school. I wanted to be able to dance and thought some of the black guys had moves that I might try to imitate, that nowadays would be called minimalist.

That's what I was after, what by this time I had appropriated and named the Nothing Dance.

If any of my young colt and filly readers want to try this one, here's what you do. You have your arms sort of down by your sides. Then when normal dancers start stepping all over the place with their legs, swinging their arms everywhere, and making their hips have a hiccup to the front or to the side, you have these different parts of your body *imagine* doing those moves, but not actually moving. The most you want to move is like when a fly lands on a horse's shoulder or rump, and he sort of shivers it off. All this unmoving should somehow correspond as much as possible to the actual rhythm and beat of the music. I confess, that's the part I had the most trouble with.

I found myself out on the dance floor doing the nothing dance, I thought with better rhythm than usual, compared to recent practice in my dorm when Tiger was not around. My partner Mary, on the other hand, was Charo, alternately doing the "cuchi-cuchi" and stopping momentarily to give a pep talk to a stand-up corpse. I was having none of it.

Then she grabbed both of my arms and swung them somehow, so she ended up standing next to me on my right, with my right arm over her shoulder holding her left hand, and my left arm at waist height holding her right hand. "Jees, what do I do now?" I'm thinking, when she suddenly spun in another direction—I can't say for sure that it was the opposite direction, but I imagine it must have been, to leave me back where I started from, where I could resume doing nothing, albeit with rhythm, or at least feigned rhythm. (In retrospect this may have prepared me for my encounter with God, because my way of dancing required me to strike just the right balance between an unmoved mover and a moved unmover.)

After several songs we got another glass of wine, this time mixed with more Sprite and ice cubes. Mary had warmed up and removed her denim jacket, I was practically sweating, definitely not from overdoing it on the dance floor, but from fear that she would think I danced like an idiot. We headed for the second floor terrace, which by now was probably colder than earlier, but felt warmer.

"Joe, I like the way you dance. It complements almost anything I feel like doing out there. It's like you're a neutral colored sofa and I'm the bold and flashy throw pillows. You're so subtle."

"You're very kind, Mary. But my unmoving hides an awful lot of unknowing."

"Okay, but anytime you feel like it, just grab my hand and spin me around."

"Sure. I'd probably end up with a dislocated shoulder and you'd spend a semester in traction."

We had a little more wine and then returned to the dance floor for part of their second set. This time they were playing soul music. And with the extra wine, my movements became ever so slightly more pronounced. When they did their version of Barry White's "Can't Get Enough of Your Love, Babe," with an extra heavy conga beat, I felt like I had a coffee percolator inside me. I had to do my best to keep it from spilling out onto the floor.

Mary was ready to go home after the Barry White song. Her mother was driving down to take her to Sunday brunch at the Nassau Inn. And I was driving down to my Nonna's in Camden on Sunday for a pasta fix. I walked her to her dorm. I don't remember how it started or who started it, but when we got to her building, I realized that we had been holding hands.

Now I was in a pickle. What should I do? So I turned

slightly toward her and kind of cupped the hand I was holding with both of my hands, and said I hoped to see her again soon, which took a lot of courage, because now in my imagination I was sure that my coffee percolator spectacle on the dance floor must have mortified her. "Maybe we could play pool together sometime. I'm curious to see how much your father taught you. I'm very patient, and I'll spot you some balls to make it fair. So don't worry about how good you are."

"That sounds nice, Joey." And with that she squeezed my hands in both of hers, leaned in and gave me a quick kiss on the lips. "Goodnight Joey Nostrils."

I walked away not knowing how I managed to put one foot in front of the other, because I was practically psychotic with ecstasy, and wonder. "What, what, did that really happen? Did she just kiss me?" I did a speed walk back to Campus Club and upstairs to the billiard room, and back down to the bar to get a glass of wine, which I had to drink before I could calm down enough to tell Tiger what just happened. I stayed up and played Nine Ball with Tiger and a couple of other guys until the band stopped playing for the night.

The Billiard Room Episode

We live in succession, in division, in parts, in particles. Meantime within man is the soul of the whole; the wise silence; the universal beauty, to which every part and particle is equally related; the eternal One.

— Ralph Waldo Emerson ("The Over-Soul")

A WEEK LATER WE HAD A SATURDAY AFTERNOON "POOL and pizza" party. Mary, Tiger, and I were all in town that day. Saturday afternoons were usually pretty quiet in the Campus Club billiard room, especially since we didn't have a party scheduled that weekend. Some of the clubs traded off Saturday parties, letting the other clubs' members join in the fun. Tiger, the architecture major, liked to play on the real billiard table, which had no pockets and required a healthy grasp of geometry to excel at it. So after picking up a take-out pizza at the Grotto, down on Witherspoon Street, and getting some wine from the fridge in the basement bar

—Tiger got a mug of beer, we went upstairs to the billiard room.

We were going to play Eight Ball and agreed that Mary and I would play first. The winner would play Tiger, and the loser could play around on the billiard table until it was his or her turn to play the winner, and so on. I had no idea how well she could play, so I chivalrously offered to spot her as many balls as she would like. Eight Ball is played with all fifteen balls. It can be played by two people or two teams. Each opponent has to sink all the low balls, one through seven, or all the high balls, nine through fifteen. Only after they sink all their balls are they allowed to sink the eight ball. If you sink the eight ball on the break, you win. If you sink it after the break, but before you sink your other balls, you lose. If you sink it after you sink your other balls, you win.

"Let's play the first game without a handicap; I might be able to hold my own. Let's just see," she said.

That was the understatement of the year. She broke the eight-ball in on the first game, so Tiger's turn to play came before he finished his first bite of pizza. Then she ran the table on Tiger.

Usually people who play that well are cocky about it. Onlookers and opponents will say that a player who's that good "shows all the signs of a misspent youth," which was a compliment where I grew up. Mary was very tentative on every shot. Although she used "english" or "shape" on the cue ball to get it in a position to make each subsequent shot very easy, she would hesitate, as though she wasn't sure exactly which ball she wanted to sink next and where she wanted to sink it. She made numerous bank shots and a massé shot, but she would have a look of surprise when they went in the pockets. She played with the demeanor and humility of a saint, looking as though it was the first time she ever laid eyes on a pool table. But she had complete and utter command of it.

"Mary, your father taught you to play like that?" Tiger asked. "Does he hustle pool for a living?"

"Father's a theologian at Columbia. He only plays at home. Father wanted to learn since high school, but my grandfather wouldn't allow it. For as long as I can remember, we had a pool table—actually a snooker table—in the basement rec room. Father said he bought it when he and Mother had our house built, shortly after they were married. When I was ten years old he taught me how to play snooker."

"That's a hard game, especially if you're nearsighted like me," I said. "The table's bigger than a pool table and the pockets are smaller."

"Our snooker table is tournament size, six by twelve feet. I've learned to adapt with my eyesight. Instead of aiming for the exact spot on the ball where I should hit, I aim for the exact spot on the blurry ball where I should hit. We can play regular pool on it as well. We play straight pool mostly. It's my favorite game."

"Wait. You're Jewish, Mary? Are you allowed to play pool on Saturdays?"

"I am and I am, Tiger. That's a good question. You must know something about Judaism. We go to a Reform synagogue. Father plays pool with me sometimes on Shabbat, I mean Saturday. Shabbat is a day for rest and relaxation. We relax by playing pool together. Mother and I are not very observant, but we try to placate Father where possible."

Straight pool is played with fifteen numbered balls and the cue ball. You can sink any ball in any order, but you must name the object ball and the pocket it's to go in, even on the break. At the end of the rack, you leave the last ball where it lies on the table. You try to leave that ball in a position—a *break* shot—that makes it easy to sink, as well as allowing the cue ball to career off it (called a carom or a kiss) to *break* open the rack for the next shot. The first person to reach a cumulative score of one hundred points—sometimes more, as agreed—wins. Each ball is worth just one point, no matter what number it is.

"We could play three-way straight pool, if you like, Mary. Tiger, how does that sound?"

"Sure," Tiger said, "we'll play to a hundred. Mary, you can spot us ninety points each."

"He's just kidding, Mary. Do you want to play straight pool?"

"Yes, sure. I'll shoot last, one of you can break."

"Oh, no, no, no, no, no," I said, "Ladies first; besides, the opening break is the hardest shot in straight pool."

"Okay, I'll break," she said.

There are two shots that can be made on the opening break; they're both very hard and very rarely attempted. The rack of fifteen balls makes an equilateral triangle, with no obvious ball and pocket to call. Over the years talented pool players learned to hit the ball on either of the two back corners in just such a way and with just the right amount of force to make it bounce (called a bank shot) off the far cushion and come all the way up the table and sink in one of the nearest corner pockets. But it's hard to do and not often successful. The other shot is even harder than that, and very rarely attempted. You hit the ball at the front of the rack— the apex ball—at just the right spot and with just the right amount of low, reverse "english" to make it spin out of its little socket and into the side pocket opposite from the side from which you shot. In billiards—pool is sometimes called pocket billiards—english is not capitalized. When you are bent over the pool table with the tip of your cue stick aiming at the cue ball, you imagine that it's a clock face. Twelve o'clock is high english, six is low, three is right, nine is left, two is high-right, ten is high-left, and so on. These primarily affect what the cue ball does *after* it hits the object ball. Players use english to position the cue ball where it will have an easy time of sinking the next ball. Reverse english is when you hit the cue ball on the opposite side from which you'll hit the object ball. Mary called the apex ball in the side pocket.

"Sure. Go ahead Mary. Humiliate us," I said.

"She can't humiliate us if no one else is here to see it," Tiger said.

"Tiger, you know I'm easily confused. Is this like the sound of one hand clapping or like the tree falling in the forest with no one to hear?"

"I don't know, Joey, but we'd better shut the door so no one else sees this."

She made the shot and made it look easy. But then she miscued (the stick accidentally slips off the cue ball) on her next shot, which caused her to lose a point and to lose her turn.

Tiger's turn was next. While he proceeded to run out the rack, leave himself an easy break shot, and then run four more balls into the next rack, for a total run of eighteen points—quite respectable, I took some rough sandpaper, kept in a drawer for this purpose, and scuffed up the tip of Mary's pool stick for her. It wasn't a personal stick that Mary brought for the occasion, but a "house" stick shared by everyone who didn't bring their own. Over time the leather tips get worn down and change from the feel of suede to that of smooth leather, making them slippery. Tiger and I had our own personal, very expensive sticks—his a McDermott and mine a Meucci (thanks to extra pay for the door repair), but they didn't help us play as well as Mary.

My turn was next. I managed to sink the rest of the rack, for ten points. But I left myself a terrible break shot and did not make it into the next rack.

Next up, the magician, that's how we thought of Mary after watching her. She came nowhere near to breaking Willie Mosconi's 1954 record of 526 shots in a row. But she ran forty-nine balls, before accidentally sinking the cue ball, a *scratch* that cost her one point and her turn.

"Mary, you are clearly out of our league," Tiger said, "But there's something strange. The balls seem to end up in a circle around the middle of the table, about halfway through every rack you've played. How do you do that? Did you see that, Joey?"

"I wasn't paying attention. But yes, what's he talking about, Mary?"

"I didn't see any funny business. I'm not saying that. It just seems strange."

"Okay, Mary, maybe it's magic. How did you do that?"

"I do notice it," she said. "But I don't do it on purpose. I think it's a spiritual sign or a message of some sort. I don't know why it's happening or what it means. But the circle is universal in the spiritual realm. In Jewish mysticism God is shown as a series of circles emanating out from *Ein Sof*, the unknowable, at the center. In the Notre-Dame de Chartres cathedral the circular Labyrinth symbolizes a spiritual pilgrimage. In the Eastern religions the circular mandalas represent our spiritual journey. Stonehenge had a series of circles of smaller stones inside the famous, larger, outer circle. The signs of the zodiac are arranged in a circle as well. I have not played pool anywhere on campus until now. But I saw this happening while playing at home. I thought it started around the time I learned about locking God in a closet. I really hadn't thought much about it until now."

"Wait, wait," Tiger interrupted, "Is your God in a closet? That's why we don't have a God; we have a One. All is One. We try to become one with the One." He was talking while shooting his turn. He did better this time, almost sinking two whole racks.

"Mary, tell Tiger about locking God in a closet," I said, as I got up for my turn. She repeated the story she told me earlier, but Tiger was having none of it.

"That sounds like your God. But our Buddha doesn't like to be in the house. He sits under a tree. Lǎolao said he's in a garden. It's our garden now, inner garden," pointing at his forehead.

"Who's Lǎolao?"

"That's his grandmother. It's not her name; it means grandmother."

"Joey's my translator, Mary. He's been my roommate only three years and he already knows five Chinese words. So we do the same, but it's a garden. We don't know flowers from weeds. So we pull flowers sometimes and plant weeds, when we think we're doing the opposite. Not on purpose, but before long we're in a briar patch. So we have to sit on our hands for a while. Meditate, until we understand where we went wrong. Try to plant no more weeds. Just plant flowers. Hard to learn the difference. Takes a long time. Many days just sitting on hands. Do nothing. But at least do no harm. One day we look around. See beautiful garden. Still have to tend it for our entire life. But now we live in beautiful garden. Buddha may come sit with us. Maybe the garden is a circle. Last year in History of Architecture class we learn about large circular ceremonial structures called Kivas built by the Anasazi Tribe in an area of northwest New Mexico called Chaco Canyon. The larger Kivas could hold several hundred people."

"We had a brief introduction to the Anasazi in a Comparative Religion class I took last semester," Mary said. "They had a spiral shape that figured prominently in their petroglyphs."

Tiger likes to walk all around as he talks. And he gesticulates a lot, not like an Italian. We like to talk with our hands. But Tiger is very dramatic. He walks around like he's Yul Brynner in *The King and I*, in a palace garden, swooping his arms around to take it all in, pointing at imaginary flowers and weeds, then pointing at me to make a point. I didn't make it through the break ball; that's my weak point in straight pool. Mary was intrigued by Tiger's story and waited until he was done before shooting.

"I like that garden story, Tiger. I think there's room for God in your garden," Mary said as she took aim.

"You can put one in there for yourself if you like," he said. "I think your pool balls are talking to you like the yarrow sticks talk to us in the *I Ching*."

"Maybe, Tiger. In the Torah decisions are sometimes made by casting lots, and they may have been sticks. But what is the circle trying to tell me? I sometimes think it's God's way of telling me that he is near."

"Or it's telling you that you're on the right path," I said. "Tiger, she's going to write her senior thesis on the nature of God."

"Well, then it could just as likely be warning her that she's on the wrong path," Tiger said. "I'll have to look more closely at the rack when I'm shooting. Maybe Lǎolao will send *me* a message."

Tiger and I made strange faces at each other and at the table as we watched Mary run the other fifty-one balls she needed to win the game. This time we were paying careful attention, trying to figure out how some of the balls seemed to gravitate to the center and form a circle in almost every rack. There wasn't anything we could see that explained it, other than what appeared to be the random way that the balls break and then get moved around the table during the game, except hers gravitate toward the center.

We had plenty of time to eat our pizza while watching Mary. After the game she suggested that Tiger and I play while she ate some pizza. We played a couple of games of Eight Ball. We're pretty evenly matched. I am probably a better shot, but I get impulsive. So I'll sometimes make a hard shot, follow it with overconfidence, and miss an easy one right afterward. Tiger's more Zenlike. His approach is closer to Mary's; he stops and thinks about every shot. Tiger had to run off, and Mary wanted to stop.

"I think it's teatime, Joe."

"Okay, sure. That sounds good," I said. "Maybe we could sit on the terrace. It's supposed to be up in the fifties this afternoon."

"That would be lovely."

We fetched our tea and then found a sunny spot on the terrace. It was early April. It was in the low fifties. I had not been paying much attention to the weather; Mary thought it was the warmest day of the year so far. And we were sitting in a spot that was sheltered from the wind.

"Don't you feel the sun giving you a big warm hug? 'Joey Nostrils,' it says, 'So lovely to see you again. I've missed you. I could see you from afar all winter, but it's so nice to get close again.'"

"Sure, but pretty soon it will be hugging every guy in the whole state."

"Well, we have it all to ourselves today. Oh, I almost forgot. When I met with Professor Kaufmann Wednesday, after the serious stuff, about my thesis and all, we were just chatting. He said that Princeton was the worst place in the world to find some skilled help for little projects around the house. I said I may have just the person, and then I told him about you. He said if you're interested he had some small projects for you."

"I might have time to look at them next weekend. I should have my thesis done by then. Did he say what they were?"

"He said his front door bottom is rotting; I think he called it a threshold. And he had two small antique mosaics that were cracking. He wondered if you knew how to fix them."

"I don't know about the mosaics. I'll have to see them. See if he wants me to look at them next weekend."

"He's a tea drinker. I'll get us invited over there for tea next Saturday afternoon. How does that sound?"

"Sure. Let me know when it's definite. What if he's doing something else that day?"

"I'll call you when I find out. It's too far to walk, but it's an easy bike ride. Do you have a bike? If not, he'll probably offer to come get us, since he's having a hard time finding a carpenter."

"I don't have a bike; I have a bug."

"A bug?"

"Yes, a VW Beetle. It's thirteen years old, but it runs all right. My father helped me get it when I started school here. Look over the railing. It's that light blue one in the corner to the left."

"Okay, Joey, what if we go in your Beetle?"

The Campus Carpenter Episode

WE MET PROFESSOR KAUFMANN FOR TEA THE following Saturday afternoon, and after we had tea with some homemade lemon cookies that Mrs. Kaufmann put out for us, he showed me the door and the mosaics.

"Professor Kaufmann, your threshold is oak. I think it rotted for two reasons, or maybe three. One, it's too flat. It needs to have a slope so rainwater and snow won't stay on it. Two, it needs a coat of varnish at least once a year. And three, a storm door would give it an extra layer of protection from the weather."

"It had a storm door; I took it off when we moved here. I like to see the wood door."

"Okay, Professor. I could make a mahogany threshold, with a better slope on it, and then protect it with several coats of a marine grade varnish, like Epifanes."

"When will you have time to do it, Joe?" he asked.

"I'm going to my parents' house in Bridgeview tomorrow for dinner. My father might have a piece of mahogany in his shop. If he does, then I can use his table saw and planer to make the threshold. And I can install it sometime during the week. If my father doesn't have any mahogany, then I'll have to get some around here. I think Hamilton Building Supply carries mahogany. I could make it next weekend in my father's shop and install it the following week."

"What would you charge me, Joe?"

"Well, Professor, there's more to it. After I get the old threshold removed, I have to check your subfloor for damage. There should be a vapor barrier over it, either tar paper or rosin paper. If that's not damaged, then the subfloor should be okay. Sometimes the vapor barrier's missing altogether, and then there could be damage to the subfloor and to the floor joists. Sometimes there's metal flashing under it, which is the best case scenario. I hope we get lucky, but I won't know until I get the old threshold out. I prefer to charge by the hour for labor, and you would reimburse me for the materials. You'll be able to see me working on it. I work hard. But I don't rush; I snipped off this thumb when I was sixteen, probably from rushing. But I work steadily. I don't dilly-dally. I won't charge you for travel time to my parents' house, because I'm going there anyway."

"Wait, Joe," Mary interrupted. "I never saw your thumb."

"Of course you didn't, because it's not there. But you know it's missing?"

"Joe, that's what I mean; I haven't noticed that it's missing."

"What? Are you serious? I carry a three-story neon sign around that says, 'Man missing a left thumb; grotesque man with no left thumb.'" (I was very self-conscious about it back then; now I hardly notice that it's missing.)

"He's funny, Mary," Professor Kaufmann said. "Okay Joe, what is your rate?"

"I charge twenty dollars an hour. I have my own tools, and my father lets me use all of his tools as well. He has everything I could possibly need."

"Now just a minute, Joe, shouldn't I get a discount for a carpenter with a missing thumb? Just teasing there, but seriously, how long do you think it will take?"

"I like to tell people what my father tells them, 'It takes what it takes.' There's always a best case scenario and a worst case scenario. If there's no damage to the subfloor or the floor joists, then maybe two to three hours to make up the new threshold in my father's shop, an hour or two to remove the old one, an hour or two to install the new one, then less than an hour, but a few trips to come and put a few coats of varnish on it. So if we're lucky, then eight to ten hours."

"And what would the worst case be?"

"I can't say. So much depends on whether the floor joists are damaged or not."

"I think we can see them in my basement. It's not finished off."

We went down to his basement and I was able to see that the floor joists were in good shape under the front door. So I told him that the worst case could be another four to six hours if I had to repair the plywood subfloor.

"That's fair, Joe. Now let's see what you think about my mosaics."

While we were in the basement talking about his repair, Mary was looking through several open cartons of some of his books that were stacked on a folding table. "I haven't seen this one," she said. "*Existentialism from Dostoevsky to Sartre*; is it in the bookstore?"

"It's for a senior class seminar on Existentialism I'll be teaching in the fall. I hope you'll sign up for it. Take a copy. Go ahead. That's a revised edition that was just published."

"I couldn't. I'll buy it in the bookstore."

"No, please. That's your reward for bringing me a carpenter."

He brought us out into the garage, where he had the two mosaics, in small wooden crates, like oversized cigar boxes, lying on a workbench. They were about a foot and a half long by about a foot wide.

I could see a long vertical crack in one, and the second was cracked across the middle, with the top half cracked into two pieces. Professor Kaufmann thought they might have come from the kitchen of an ancient Roman house, because they had a tessellated pattern commonly used in Roman houses around the first century AD.

"A colleague in the archaeology department said that the mortar back then was likely lime, clay, sand and possibly some volcanic ash."

"My uncle Lou gave me a big lecture on mortar mixes when I told him I might have to fix some old mosaics. He's a union plasterer in Philly. He says nowadays the cement has fly ash from burning coal; it does the same thing as the volcanic ash. He said regular mason's mortar mix has what I need, but to look at the mortar behind your mosaics to see how sandy it is. I need to make my mix about as sandy as the original mix looks, but a minimum ratio of three to one, sand to mortar mix. It's not an exact science. He said to reinforce it with some lath, or chicken wire. I would make a form to pour it in, with the mosaics upside down. He said at least as thick as the original mortar, but three quarters of an inch minimum. If the original mortar is kind of sandy and porous, then he said I should use a slurry mix as a bonding agent. Plaster bonds to old plaster and other masonry surfaces by a process called "suction." The dryer material tries to suck the moisture out of the wetter material until they're in balance, which helps them to bond to one another. I have to moisten the original mortar just the right amount—too little and it will suck too much moisture from the new plaster, ruining the mix; too much and they won't bond. But if the original mortar is kind of hard and not very porous, then I'll use Weld-Crete, a bonding agent they use to bond stucco to concrete. I hope that doesn't sound too complicated, because there's more to it. After it's done, it needs to be misted with water once or twice a day for several days, to "moist-cure," which makes it stronger. It will just take a few minutes each time. You can mist it yourself, or I can come by and do it if needed. I can't say how long it will last, but the new plaster will be solid and the metal lath will keep it from cracking again."

Over the next several weeks I was able to find a few hours here and there to complete both projects. They went smoothly, and I was lucky that the threshold rot did not spread into the subfloor. The professor was pleased with the overall cost, and as a bonus he gave me about a half dozen of his books. I started to read them over that summer.

The Picnic Preparation Episode

"Angels can fly because they take themselves lightly."

— Written on a paperweight in a gift shop.

WHEN WE LEFT PROFESSOR KAUFMANN'S IT WAS almost time for the clubs to start serving dinner, so I dropped Mary off at Stevenson and went straight to Campus Club. She had a paper due that Monday, so she wasn't interested in any partying, but she suggested that we plan a picnic lunch down at Lake Carnegie soon. Lake Carnegie was at the far east end of the campus, at the bottom of a gently rolling hill whose top was at Nassau Street, the west end of the campus. When I dropped her off, she leaned over and kissed me, saying, "I really like you, Joey."

Now I was getting a little nervous. To be truthful, I was speechless from nervousness.

"Let's have tea at your club Monday afternoon," she said. "We can plan a picnic for next weekend."

"I'm sorry darling, my father is framing an addition to

our house next weekend and it's all hands on deck. I'm afraid I'll be in Bridgeview all weekend. The following weekend is good."

"Did you just call me darling?" she said.

Uh oh. Now I ruined it. "I wasn't thinking straight. It just came out. I meant you're *a* darling, not *my* darling, nothing like that, I mean I treasure our friendship. I don't mean that I couldn't fall in love with you and all in a New York second, or maybe I am already, I mean. But I'm really talking myself into a pretzel. I should shut up. I should probably never open my mouth."

"Joey, it was very sweet; it gave me goosebumps."

"What? What? I'm giving *you* goosebumps? That is just crazy, because when I see you my feet practically leave the ground. And when you kiss me I almost faint from happiness." Now I leaned over to kiss *her*, clumsily as all-get-out, to borrow a phrase from Mark Twain. But it worked in spite of my awkwardness. Now I really went for broke, just blurting it out in spite of Tiger's warning, "Would you say that we are dating?"

"I think you could say that, Joey. Is Monday at three o'clock okay? We can plan a picnic for two Saturday's from now."

"Yes, Monday at three is good; that's a date," I said. I'm not sure if I said that's a date.

On Monday afternoon I had some time to work on the wooden forms I was making for Professor Kaufmann's mosaics. Mrs. Kaufmann let me into the garage. I was a little too absorbed in the work and didn't get to Campus Club until a few minutes after Mary. She was sitting on the living room couch under the front window and writing in a notepad.

"Mary, I'm so sorry I'm late. I was working on the

mosaics at Professor Kaufmann's and forgot to check my watch. Want some tea?"

"I helped myself," she said, pointing to her cup on the coffee table.

"Oh, great. I'll just get myself some coffee," I said.

When I sat down I didn't want to sit so close that I would seem presumptuous. But I didn't want her to think I lost interest either. So first I sat down about a foot away from her. Then I shimmied a little closer, then a little farther, then closer, then farther.

She finally yanked me over to her by the elbow, saying, "Look at this list I'm making for our picnic. What do you think?"

"I like the wine and 7-UP. Let me see. Okay. Cheese, crackers, grapes, rolls. Sure. I guess we can get all this at the grocery store. Do you want to just get a couple of subs from Hoagie Haven?"

"Oh, no. Preparing the food ourselves is an important part of the picnic. This ritual has been performed by couples for centuries. After all, we are dating now," she said as she lightly brushed the back of my hair with her hand.

"And we're a couple too?"

"Well, Joey, almost. To officially be a couple, we would have to recite poems to each other. You can write a poem to read to me, and I'll write one for you."

"Uh oh. I knew this was too good to be true. I'm a horrible writer, and I've never written a poem. I wouldn't know where to start, especially with a love poem. Can I just find one to read to you?"

"No, not a love poem, Joey. You can bring any poem that you like. But you should write one as well, even if it's short. Professor Kaufmann said that writing is a way to examine your thoughts more clearly than you could while they are swirling around in your head. He compared the act of writing something on paper to film editing, where you could view your thoughts in slow motion, freeze-frame them, and even reverse the film, making changes as you see fit. So it's only by writing that you become good at writing. And as a by-product you become a better thinker as well."

"I think in my case the more I write the worse it becomes. Did I tell you that I'm a "C" student? I'm not very smart."

"Joey, you didn't get into Princeton by accident. Surely you can write a few lines of poetry."

"I think I did get in by accident. Tiger said I was probably a 'hay-fever' admit. They make these decisions in the spring. The dean of admission probably had hay fever and sneezed just as she was ready to set my application on the reject pile, and it blew over onto the acceptance pile."

"Come on, Joey. You know that's not true."

"Well, if I'm going to write a poem, it would have to be an assignment. Make believe you're the professor and tell me what to write about."

"Okay, let me think. Oh, I got it; write something that you would consider spiritual. Maybe you're a transcendentalist, like Emerson or Thoreau, or a humanist."

"Or maybe I'm a utilitarian, like John Stuart Mill. I really haven't given it much thought."

"You're in good company, Joey. Nietzsche thinks all systems of thought are flawed, and some fatally, especially religion."

"That's good to know. Then would Nietzsche consider a poem a system? Because mine will be severely flawed."

"Joey, I don't think a poem is a system. I guess it could be. But most aren't. I think the best poems are enigmatic, not systematic. Besides, chaos theory would say that even if your writing starts out disorganized, if you just keep writing, eventually it will reorganize itself on a higher level. That's called the bifurcation point."

"That's the key phrase here, 'it will reorganize *itself*,' because I certainly can't reorganize it on a higher level. It will have to magically do it on its own, preferably when I'm asleep. Besides, aren't Kaufmann and your chaos theory stuff really just saying that practice makes perfect?"

"They are. But they are also telling us *how* practice makes perfect."

"All right then, can I write something spiritual if I don't believe in God?"

"Joey, you must know you can, after rooming with Tiger for almost three years. Wouldn't you agree that Buddhist monks are spiritual? Nietzsche doesn't believe in God, but in many ways one can say that his quest for truth is a spiritual quest."

"I don't know enough about Nietzsche. I like what Turgenev said, that truth is like a lizard. No sooner you grab its tail, it scurries off and grows a new one."

"That's funny, Joey. Did he really say that?"

"I think he did. I have a lot of books swirling around in my head."

"I guess you do. Have you ever read anything by Paul Tillich? He speaks about God and faith, but for him God is not a being, but the source of all being, and faith is not an answer to questions about the meaning of life, but the quest to find the answers, even if you're an atheist."

"I never heard of him. It sounds like semantic smoke and mirrors to me. Isn't his 'source of all being' just a higher order being itself?"

"It just might be, Joey. And I am not too familiar with how he looks at that. I just wanted to mention that according to him, questions about the meaning of life should be our 'ultimate concern.' If we make anything else our ultimate concern, it will end in despair. That's my ulterior motive for suggesting something spiritual. I'm on that quest. And I'm curious to see how you'll react to the subject of spirituality."

"So this is a test. What if I fail miserably? Will we still be dating?"

"Joey, stop that. It is not a test. Anything you bring gets an A plus for exposing your soul."

"What if I don't have a soul? Can you just grade on a pass or fail? If I bring a poem I pass?"

"You don't have to have a soul; you can have a psyche, or an inner being."

"Maybe it's a Freudian subconscious, or Jungian."

The Picnic Episode

I have lived on the lip
of insanity, wanting to know reasons,
knocking on a door. It opens.
I've been knocking from the inside!

— Rumi

TWO SATURDAYS LATER WE MET IN FRONT OF MARY'S
dorm and walked together to Campus Club, where we had
stashed the picnic food that we bought at the grocery store
after dinner Friday night. I borrowed a small cooler from
the bar to use as a picnic basket, which we loaded into the
VW's trunk. We drove down to the Lake Carnegie parking
lot on Faculty Road, then found a comfortable spot on the
grass near the water to spread out a blanket that Mary
brought from her dorm in a big white canvas tote bag.

It was a beautiful afternoon. It was already above
seventy and supposed to go up to the mid-seventies. It was
mostly cloudy, but I remember that the clouds were

beautiful. Mary wanted to just lie on the blanket for a few minutes to stare up at the clouds. There was a large Weeping Willow tree nearby that was covered in these pretty yellow flowers, which looked especially colorful against the grey sky.

"Pour us a glass of wine, Joey, and a splash of soda, please. It's a lovely day, isn't it?"

"We couldn't ask for a better day."

We weren't celebrating Memorial Day or even thinking about it; but the grocery store already had the red, white and blue plastic dinnerware kits on sale. So I poured our wine into red plastic glasses, along with some aged provolone cheese on a white plastic plate, and a couple of navy blue napkins. "Mary, I hope you'll like this cheese. It's nothing like the sliced provolone they put on sandwiches. It's sharp, almost like grated cheese."

She took a bite and smiled. "I do like it, Joey." Then she giggled. "Although I must say, there's something hilariously incongruous about having red, white and blue dinnerware at a romantic picnic."

"I was kind of thinking that too," I said. We nibbled on our cheese and sipped our wine, while looking out at the lake. There was a light breeze and it gave the water a light chop. The sun would show itself from time to time, but even through the clouds it made the top of each ripple glisten bright white over a dark valley floor. It was like watching thousands of miniature snow-capped mountains forming and dissolving before your eyes. "I get so hypnotized watching the water," I said.

"Me too, Joey. I have the same feeling watching fire. I can sit and stare at the fireplace forever." We were sitting together on the blanket, with the plate between us. She slid it forward, and then turning slightly to the side she leaned her shoulder onto my chest. This gave me the warmest feeling. "Did you bring me a poem, Joey?"

"I did, but can we just sit here like this a few more minutes?"

"Of course we can; you feel very cozy."

"This feels very romantic and I want to savor it before reading a decidedly unromantic poem. I don't even think it's a poem. It's a schedule."

"A schedule? Read it to me while we sit here like this. I'm curious."

"No, I'm kind of embarrassed now. I don't think it's what you had in mind."

"Come on, Joey. You get an A+ for bringing it. Read it to me."

With that I reached into my back pocket and pulled out the folded yellow paper with my schedule slash poem. "I think this will convince you that I really did get into Princeton by accident, that I really was a hay-fever admit," I said as I unfolded the paper and started to read.

Another Day in Paradise (My *Trillionth* Day)

Six AM - Prayer Breakfast.
Seven AM – Trumpet Practice.
Eight AM – Choir Practice.
Nine AM – Polish God's Throne. (Why did I volunteer for this?)
Ten AM - Pearly Gate Trumpet Duty.
Eleven AM – Bake Casserole.

Noon – Neighborhood Potluck Casserole Luncheon.
One PM – Praise God.
Two PM – Worship God.
Three PM – Contemplate God.

Four PM – Anoint God's Feet With Oil.
Five PM – Make Meatballs.

Six PM – Neighborhood Potluck Spaghetti Supper.
Seven PM - Induction in Trillionaires Club for saying
Rosary daily (Shema if Jewish, Chant OM if Buddhist).
Eight PM – Choir Recital at God's Throne (two hours).
Ten PM – Maybe I can get some sleep. (Oops, almost forgot
to say the Rosary.)
After a trillion days or so, they say you start to fall into a
routine.
Do other people get bored here, or is it just me?

"That's funny, Joey. It makes me think about eternity. How long is it? Is it a trillion times a trillion years? Or does that even scratch the surface of an eternity?"

"I don't think it scratches the surface, Mary. I don't think a quadrillion times a quadrillion years scratches the surface of an eternity. Who came up with this idea that we'd want to live in a pearly-gated neighborhood forever and ever and ever? Or is it a big city? It boggles the mind. I don't really believe this stuff. But there's a little Catholic boy somewhere inside me who does."

"Jewish ideas about the afterlife are very diverse. But rest assured, if there's a paradise for us, we will have bagels and lox." With that we both laughed.

"It's your turn now," I said.

Mary reached into her tote bag for a black and white composition notebook. "Are you ready, Joey?" And then she read.

Trees
Their friendships
Endure for centuries.
Their boughs shelter
Neighbors' saplings
From summer storms.
And sometimes
They become lovers,
When their branches
Intertwine.

"Mary, I think I wish I were a tree now."

"Do you wish our branches would intertwine, Joey?" she said, while pulling my arms out from behind me—I had them propping me up like a tripod. I'm not sure how she did it, but now she was lying on top of me with her arms tucked under mine and hugging me, with her warm cheek on my cheek.

I was panting like I just climbed several flights of stairs, more from nervousness than anything. She wasn't heavy at all. Imagine two toothpicks stacked together, or it was more like a female praying mantis jumping on top of a male praying mantis, about to decapitate him. No, it wasn't that scary, but I was such a klutz (I still am) that I was extremely worried about where to put my arms and legs. I felt ecstatic lying like that and scared to death at the same time that I would accidentally do something wrong. So I thought the safest thing to do was to stay perfectly still.

In that delightful, albeit awkward position, I tried to answer her question, but my voice quivered like it did in childhood when my father made some embarrassing outburst in church. I think the little, and to be truthful, very neurotic Catholic boy in me was afraid someone would see us and think that we were doing something that we weren't. "I think the trees live a much more noble life than humans; your poem strikes at the heart of it, and beautifully so." My voice was audibly shaking.

"Thank you, Joey, that was very sweet. Okay, did you bring a poem to read? It's your turn," she said, as she perched herself up on her folded knees beside me.

"I did. I was in the poetry aisles at Firestone Library and I stumbled upon a poem that reminds me of your God-locked-in-the-closet story. It's by Rainer Maria Rilke; I never heard of him. I stumbled upon almost everything I've ever read unless it was a school assignment. I don't find the things I read; I think they somehow find me. I checked this book out of the library." Then I read it to Mary.

You, Neighbor God

You, God, who live next door—
If at times, through the long night, I trouble you
with my urgent knocking—
this is why: I hear you breathe so seldom.
I know you're all alone in that room.
If you should be thirsty, there's no one
to get you a glass of water.
I wait listening, always. Just give me a sign!
I'm right here.
As it happens, the wall between us
is very thin. Why couldn't a cry
from one of us
break it down? It would crumble easily.
It would barely make a sound.

— Rainer Maria Rilke

"Joey, where did you find that poem? I can't wait to share it with my friend from the synagogue. It's not the same story as hers, but somehow it resonates with hers. It sounds like God is treating the narrator like Rabbi Saunders treated his eldest son, Danny in *The Chosen*."

"I never read that."

"The Rabbi deliberately raised Danny in silence so Danny would know what it is like to suffer, in his case, loneliness, so that Danny would have compassion for others, because Danny was supposed to become his successor. What a beautiful poem; so here God is keeping silent like the Rabbi."

"I know nothing about this poem or the author. It says it's translated from German. But when I saw it I knew it was for you. It doesn't speak to me. Maybe in a negative sense, because when I was twelve years old in confirmation class, the nun told us that we are supposed to love our neighbor as ourselves. And then she told us that our neighbor was the stranger, like the Samaritan in the Bible. She thought this was important, and she harped on us from another angle. She told us the Bible said, 'How can you love God, whom you cannot see, if you don't love your brother, whom you can see?' So I blurted out, 'Then we're pretty stupid, because God made the strangers in all different colors so it would be easier to recognize them in order to love them, but we see the different colors as something to hate.' The nun was angry with me for not raising my hand, but not for what I said."

"The Torah speaks to that same question, Joey. Leviticus 19:18 says to love your neighbor as yourself. And Leviticus 19:34 says to treat the foreigner as you treat the native-born, for you were foreigners in Egypt. Now I will read something that I chose for you. It's from Goethe's

"Prometheus." There are six or seven stanzas, depending on how you count. But I am just going to read part of it. Prometheus is a Greek god who stole fire from Zeus and the other gods and gave it to humanity. He was sentenced to eternal torture by Zeus. The poem expresses his anger at Zeus and the other Greek gods, but it could express our feelings toward God."

Prometheus (Stanzas 2, 3, 4 and 5)

I know of nothing more wretched
Under the sun than you gods!
Meagerly you nourish
Your majesty
On dues of sacrifice
And breath of prayer.
And would suffer want
But for children and beggars,
Poor hopeful fools.
Once too, a child,
Not knowing where to turn,
I raised bewildered eyes
Up to the sun, as if above there were
An ear to hear my complaint,
A heart like mine
To take pity on the oppressed.

Who helped me
Against the Titans' arrogance?
Who rescued me from death,
From slavery?
Did not my holy and glowing heart,
Unaided, accomplish all?
And did it not, young and good,

Cheated, glow thankfulness
For its safety to him, to the sleeper above?

I pay homage to you? For what?
Have you ever assuaged
Have you ever relieved
The burdened man's anguish?
The frightened man's tears?
Was it not omnipotent Time
That forged me into manhood,
And eternal Fate,
My masters and yours?

— Johann Wolfgang von Goethe

"What do you think, Joe? Is God dead, like Nietzsche said, or is he just asleep?"

"Or does he simply not exist? Maybe he's giving us the silent treatment, like the Rabbi gave his son in that book you mentioned."

"*The Chosen*? Yes. My grandfather—dear Zayde—said this poem expressed his own anger toward God because of the Holocaust."

"Was his name Zayde?"

"No, Joey. I'm sorry; that's Yiddish. It's like saying Nonno, or Pop-Pop, or Grandpop."

"What was his name then?"

"Benjamin. Doctor Benjamin Malin. He died last year. He had this poem taped on his refrigerator."

"Gee. People put photos of their kids and grandkids on their refrigerator. Your grandfather must have been pretty mad at God."

"Joey, look," she pointed toward the water. "A mama duck swimming with her baby ducklings."

"I'm nearsighted, but it looks like at least a half a dozen," I said as they disappeared behind the willow tree.

"There were seven, Joey. They were so cute."

"Do you want to walk along the water and follow them?"

"No, not now. I want to tell you about my Zayde. There were photos of his granddaughters on the fridge, me and my cousin Becky, he has two grandchildren. I'm sure Bubby, my grandmother, put the photos there. Zayde said everyone sees your refrigerator, including God—and he wanted God to see that poem every day. He wanted God to be ashamed of the Holocaust; he should not have let it happen. People said it proved that God was dead, or that there was no God. Zayde said that God existed, but Zayde was ashamed of God. He said if he were ever face to face with God that he would scold him until he *wished* he were dead."

"I would have liked your grandfather, Mary. I see stuff all the time that makes me think that God's an idiot, if there *is* a God. But the Holocaust, yes, I'd say he's a real idiot, a jerk, a real jerk."

"Don't say that, Joey. We don't know. There's an everyday idea of God as some sort of grandfatherly figure. But Professor Kaufmann pointed out in his *Critique* that Judaism never had an official definition for God. It's open to interpretation. My grandfather saw him in that everyday way. But I see him in charge of a vast universe. I don't know if he ever intervened, or if he could. I think he's just *there*."

"Maybe he's too old to intervene, like a very elderly grandparent who's unable to get around anymore, or even unable to speak."

"Maybe that's true, Joey. There are so many plausible

explanations out there that cannot be proven or disproven. But just one of them, if any, can be true. Have you read Dostoevsky's *The Brothers Karamazov?*"

"I read part of it. Mary. I may have mentioned before that I am a very distracted reader. If it's a class assignment, I'll read a whole book. But most of the time, I'll find a book interesting, but get distracted by another book and start reading that. Sometimes I go back to finish the first book and sometimes I don't. I remember there were two or three brothers and one was a monk."

"That's right. His name was Alyosha. His older brother, Ivan, was an atheist. Ivan told Alyosha about several extreme instances of man's inhumanity to man. One involved an aristocrat who let a pack of his hunting dogs chase and tear an eight-year-old serf boy to pieces because the boy threw a stone that accidentally hurt the paw of the aristocrat's favorite hunting dog. This spectacle was performed in front of the boy's mother and the entire village. Ivan thought that the devil, not God, created man in *his* image, or if the devil did not exist, that man invented the devil and made him in man's image. Comparing man to beasts, he said, was an insult to the beasts, since man was the only species that tortured its victims. What did John Stuart Mill say, Joey, something about God creating us knowing full well that most of us would burn for an eternity in a hell that he also created? It's just as likely that we were created in *that* God's image, and that if he doesn't exist, that we created both him and the devil in *our* image. Of course Jews don't believe in the Christian hell."

"Freud thinks that we created God in our image. If there is a real God, then he should have had a recall, like the car manufacturers, 'Nazis returned to the factory to repair defective brains that make them think it's okay to murder six million innocent people.' Can I pour you more wine?"

"No, I had enough, Joey. I have a slight headache; it happens when I think about Zayde. He sent my grandmother and Father to America before the war, in 1937. Father was eight years old. That was forty years ago, and Father says he still remembers happy times from his childhood in Berlin. Zayde said he could not in good conscience leave his patients in the middle of their treatment. He intended to wind his practice down and join Bubby and Father in America in a matter of months. But it turned out to be eight years."

"Eight years! How many patients did he have? Did you say eight years?"

"More new patients came to him, and he didn't have the heart to refuse to treat them. He made some progress toward the goal of leaving Berlin. But he was arrested and sent to a concentration camp, Sachsenhausen, the following November. He was one of just a few thousand survivors from that camp. He was freed at the end of the war, in April of 1945."

"November of 1938, was that the Kristallnacht? I read about it in high school history class."

"Yes, Joey, that was it. My striped beret was part of Zayde's uniform in the concentration camp."

"Why would he want to keep a part of a prison uniform from that place? If I were him, I'd want to forget that experience as soon as I could."

"You're right, Joey. But he was sick with a fever, very weak and emaciated when the camp was liberated. He had not been outside the barracks for almost two weeks. He wanted to hang onto the beret to protect his eyes from the sun. It somehow made the trip with him to America. I found it years later in a trunk in Bubby and Zayde's attic. I wear it sometimes. It's my silent protest against Holocaust deniers, my protest, my protest," her voice trailed off. She leaned against my shoulder and looked away—downstream.

I thought maybe she was looking for the ducks, but then I could hear her quietly sobbing. I put my arm around her and held her hand. There was nothing more to say. Finally, she turned and said she was ready to go back to her dorm. We didn't say anything while driving. But when I dropped her off, she kissed me passionately. Even as a novice in that area, I could see that our dating had crossed some major threshold. "Joey Nostrils," she said, "I think we're a couple now."

The Trip Planning Episode

The Beatific Vision, Sat Chit Ananda, Being-Awareness-Bliss, for the first time I understood, not on the verbal level, not by inchoate hints or at a distance, but precisely and completely what those prodigious syllables referred to.

— Aldous Huxley (The Doors of
Perception)

DURING THE NEXT SEVERAL WEEKS WE MET FOR afternoon coffee and tea only a few times. Mary had to finish her junior thesis. And we both had final exams and several term papers to complete. My last final exam of the semester was Monday, May 16, and Mary's last one was that Tuesday morning. We met Tuesday afternoon at Campus Club for a little celebration. "I'm ready for a glass of wine," I said. "How about you?"

"I'll have one too. Put a little extra soda in mine, please. I hope you'll take a walk with me afterwards. It would really help me to clear my head after all the studying. Besides, there's something important I want to talk about."

"Of course I'll marry you, if that's what you want to talk about." She looked at me strangely. "I'm joking, you know I'm joking. I mean I'm plum crazy about you. But that was a joke."

"You're right about being plum crazy, Joey. But I'm quite fond of you in spite of that. Let's go downstairs and have that glass of wine."

After we finished our wine, I said, "Where do you want to walk?"

"Would you mind if we took a long walk, down to Lake Carnegie and along the lake for a while?"

"Okay, sure." So we went out the basement door in the bar and started walking. The lake was straight down Washington Road, a little more than half a mile away. I remember she commented about how beautiful all the trees looked with their spring leaves in all different shades of green. It was partly cloudy, with the temperature nearing eighty degrees. "It feels good to be outside. I've been holed up in my dorm and the library studying the last several weeks," I said.

"Why don't you study outside, Joey? My friends and I spread blankets on the grass and study in Holder Courtyard."

"I tried studying on the second floor terrace at Campus Club after lunch a couple of times when the weather was nice. But I ended up playing pool both times, too many distractions there. So I usually high tail it out of there and head to the library the minute I finish eating, except after dinner. Tiger and I allowed ourselves one hour a day, after dinner, to play pool. Not this weekend. Tiger finished all his work Friday and already left for Hong Kong."

"Oh, that might come in handy for my plan."

"What plan? What do you have in mind, darling?" I

said, as I squeezed her hand a little tighter. Now half joking and half nervous, I tripped over a hump in the sidewalk created by a large tree root. Holding Mary's hand tight at just the right moment probably saved me, because she yanked me back from the start of a fall.

"No, Joey, not *that*, this," she said, as she reached inside her purse and handed me Huxley's book. "I want to do what Huxley did. It's research for my senior thesis."

"What are you talking about, Mary? I read the page with the Bergson reference, but then I had to go find where Bergson said it. Professor Jaynes is pretty fussy about making us go find the original sources. I never got back to Huxley's book. What did he do?"

"He took mescaline. It's what the Native Americans take to help them experience God, whom they call the Great Spirit."

"Do you mean the Indians? I've heard of mescaline. I thought the Indians took peyote."

"Mescaline is the active ingredient in peyote. My girlfriend Amy is at Berkeley. She has some Native American friends. They don't like to be called Indians. The name came about because Columbus thought he made it to the Indian Ocean. At first they were just called Indians. Then later they were called American Indians to distinguish them from East Indians. Native Americans, especially in our generation, feel that Indians is derogatory and racist, not to mention based on a geographical error. Some of them prefer to be called Native Peoples, because America was named after an Italian explorer, Amerigo Vespucci."

"Should I call them Native Americans then, or Native Peoples?"

"It's complicated, Joey. America is known throughout

the world as the United States of America. If a Native American travels overseas, he needs a United States of America passport. While the Native People idea is well intended, it doesn't convey *where* you're from. Amy's friends prefer to be called Native Americans, but they don't speak for the entire race."

"Wow, I had no idea. We played cowboys and Indians when I was a kid. But I always liked Tonto. It just seemed like he knew more about everything than the Lone Ranger. I was glad when my friends asked me to be the Indian. Oh, I'm sorry, I mean the Native American. I wanted to be like Tonto."

"Amy was able to send me two pills. Will you take one with me this Saturday?"

"Yikes. Is that what you wanted to talk about? Some friends from high school took LSD at an Alice Cooper concert two summers ago. It was at a baseball stadium in Jersey City. They invited me to be the designated driver. My friend Adam, who's very straight, thought that Alice Cooper was flirting with him from the stage. You know Alice Cooper is a man, don't you?"

"Who doesn't know Alice Cooper, Joey."

"Well, we were out in the far left field, about the length of a football field away from the stage, in a wall to wall crowd of people, yet Adam was sure that Alice Cooper had singled him out. He was wearing what looked like girl's leather hot pants for this one song, and Adam lost it. We had to take him out to the car until he calmed down. He wasn't ready to go back in until the concert was over. The other two guys were pissed, no pun intended, because Adam drank several beers to calm down and peed himself in the back seat. They flipped a coin to decide who had to sit on the back seat with Adam. But the whole car smelled like urine, even with the windows wide open. We had to drive all the way back to Camden from Jersey City. I had to leave that seat to air out in my parents' back yard in Bridgeview for a month. I don't think I'd want to try any psychedelics."

"Joey, just please read this book. It's only eighty pages. Mescaline is very mellow compared to LSD. Native Americans have been using it for centuries, if not longer, and they say it brings them closer to the Great Spirit. Huxley experienced something similar. It has a name, the *Mysterium Tremendum et Fascinans*, something numinous and mysterious that scares you and fascinates you at the same time. People who are actual mystics, no matter what their belief, describe that feeling when in the presence of God, or the *All* in Eastern religions. This has to be included in my research on the nature of God, if I'm to leave no stone unturned."

"You're going to leave no stone unturned for sure, but not the stones you think. They'll be rocks, lots of them, that you'll be breaking with a sledgehammer, if you get caught and sent to prison. My father said one of his uncles was in there so long that they had his name written on his sledgehammer."

"Stop it, Joey. I tried pot once in high school. I didn't care for it. I have zero interest in using any drugs, except this one, just this one time and—honestly, Joey—just because it's so important for my thesis. If you don't want to take it with me, I still very much want you to stay with me while I take it."

"I'm worried that you'll become some crazed mescaline addict; and then you'll end up on heroin."

"Joey, just read the book, please. And let me know by

Friday. I want to be able to see the stars and it's supposed to be partly cloudy Saturday night."

"You want to take the mescaline outside? Isn't that dangerous?"

"Think about it, Joey; your friends took LSD at an outdoor concert. Mescaline is a lot milder. That's why I wanted to walk here, along the lake. I'm scouting out a good clearing without too much light from nearby streetlamps or buildings, so I can see the stars. But we also need to have a safe place where we can be alone if needed, and then to sleep it off. My roommate is still here. It wouldn't be fair to her for me to come in ready to go to sleep just when she's waking up."

"Mary, I hope this isn't a dumb question. How can you see stars if you can't see well enough to drive?"

"That's a good question. I can't see them clearly if I look straight at them. I can see them if I look slightly to the side. But the slightest movement of my eyes makes them appear and disappear from my field of vision. I can see really well with binoculars. When they're slightly out of adjustment and normal viewers see double, I actually see one object."

"We have that FitzRandolph Observatory, but I don't know anything about who can use it or when they can use it." I was so disturbed by our conversation that I wasn't paying attention to our surroundings. Now I could see that we had been walking in the grass along the lake for at least a half mile.

"A friend from Stevenson knows about it. But I would have to take a guided tour, and that's too complicated. I just want to see the stars from the ground."

"I'm not going to let you lie on the ground out here by the lake in the middle of the night alone," I said. "I'll definitely stay with you. I'll read the book before I decide whether to take the mescaline myself."

"Joey, can you smell the Lilac? There's the tree," she said while pointing toward a tree by the road. "Isn't it beautiful?"

"I thought that was your perfume. I was wondering why I didn't notice it before. And I've been debating myself, should I tell you how much I like your perfume now, or is it too late? Should I have said something earlier? But I didn't smell it until now."

"Well, you're off the hook, Joey. I hardly ever wear perfume. I think this is the spot. I wonder how the Lilac will smell in the middle of the night on mescaline."

"So don't we have to plan this all out? Should we walk or drive to the lake?"

"It depends on whether you take it with me and then how you would feel about driving."

"If I take it I should probably not drive."

"Joey, it's not only a short book; the pages are small as well. Could you read forty pages tonight and forty pages tomorrow night? Then we could get together Thursday afternoon and work out the details based on whether or not you will take the other pill. We could have a picnic again, or we could just get sandwiches from Hoagie Haven and eat them on your club terrace, or anywhere you like."

Thursday we met in front of the library to walk up Nassau Street to Hoagie Haven together. This time I got to carry some books for Mary. She was already well into her research on her senior thesis. "Now I'm really worried," I said, "Are you the only student doing this much work on your senior thesis this early, or am I the only student who still doesn't have a thesis topic?"

"I bet you're not the only one, Joey. Have you finished the book? Did you decide yet?"

"I'm not quite finished, but I am going to take it with you. One reason is so that you won't be tempted to do it twice."

"You don't have to worry about that. I've thought about this carefully. I have a very good reason to take it once, but really no reason to take it more than once. So now we can plan our evening."

We got our hoagies—mine Italian, Mary's tuna salad—and headed to Campus Club. We got a large glass of water, to share, from the pantry and then headed to the second floor terrace. It was a warm, late-spring afternoon, in the high seventies, but with a nice breeze and not many clouds. "So, here's my first question: should we take it back in my room and wait for it to take effect before we walk to the lake, or should we take it after we get to the lake?"

She had just taken a bite of her hoagie, so she held up an index finger, the universal sign for "hold a second while I finish chewing."

So I said, "Okay, here's some more stuff to think about. Should we wait until it's dark out to take it, or take it right after dinner and then wait until dark to walk to the lake? Should we take our jackets and a blanket to the lake? It's supposed to go up to eighty today, but it's in the high forties to low fifties just before dawn. Saturday will be about the same. Will we stay there all night and fall asleep there, or go back to our dorms? Did you say you want to sleep in my room? You can have my bed and I'll sleep in Tiger's bed. Or you can take Tiger's bed, whichever you prefer." With that I started on my hoagie.

"Let's eat, and then we'll tackle all these details," she said.

I agreed by grunting, "Mm-hmm," through a mouthful of hoagie, while nodding my head yes.

"We could be awake for the entire night," she said after finishing her sandwich. "I think we should take it in your dorm room, after dinner, so we have time to see how it makes us feel, before we head to the lake. There's no need to go to the lake before dusk, maybe around eight-thirty or nine. I'll bring my big tote bag to carry a blanket, jackets and some water to drink. They say you don't really have an appetite on it, so I'm not bringing any food. And of course I'll bring my binoculars to look at the moon and stars."

"I can't see stars through binoculars. They look so tiny, I can't even find them. I did see the moon through them once. Last night I was at the Annex with Professor Jaynes and Stevan until around ten. I didn't see the moon walking back to my dorm."

"Have you seen it walking before? How fast does the moon walk?" she asked with a smile.

"Oh, you got me there. I was doing the walking. So I don't know what phase it's in. If it's a full moon Saturday, will that make it hard to see the stars?"

"I just want to see into space. There's plenty of sky to do that even with the moon. But I checked. It's going to be a waxing crescent moon on Saturday. It will set around eleven o'clock. The sky will be pretty dark after that. If it gets too cold later that night, we may have to scurry back to your dorm and stare at chair legs like Huxley did."

"Or we can stare at the folds in the army blanket that Tiger rigged up as drapery. He takes afternoon naps. That will come in handy if we're going to fall asleep at five or six in the morning. Huxley said that the mere folds of his flannel trousers took on infinite significance when he stared at them. Anything he stared at seemed to have some profound meaning beyond itself."

"The line that has me most curious was when he said you could see 'the All in every *this*,' that you could see in every *single* thing the divine source of all existence."

"Did Huxley get that idea from Tillich, or did Tillich get his 'source of all being' from Huxley?"

"I don't know; they're contemporaries."

"I don't think I'll see any of that anyway. I'm doing it for you, and because I'll want to know what you are experiencing at any given moment through the night. Didn't he also say that in some ways it mimics schizophrenia? We'll both be a couple of crazy people. How long did he say it lasts, a few hours? I recall him saying that for a few hours he could feel what it's like to be William Blake, so maybe it lasts a few hours."

"He said that what it shared with schizophrenia is a dreamlike state. He also said it had similarities with the mindset of geniuses, mystics and visionaries. I read somewhere that all geniuses are mad. Maybe it will turn us into geniuses, I mean *mad* geniuses. Amy told me that it would last seven or eight hours, and that it was helpful to have a glass of wine or something when you're ready to go to sleep. She said you start to feel tired long before you're able to fall asleep."

"It sounds like Amy tried it herself."

"I think you're right. But I didn't ask her and she didn't say."

"I'm out of my grandfather's wine, but I'll buy us a bottle of Chianti to have on hand for Saturday."

The Trip to the Moon Episode

One does not only wish to be understood when one writes; one wishes just as surely not to be understood. It is not by any means necessarily an objection to a book when anybody finds it impossible to understand: perhaps that was part of the author's intention—he did not want to be understood by just "anybody."

— Nietzsche (Aphorisms)

WE WAITED UNTIL IT WAS ALMOST DARK TO LEAVE MY dorm room and wend our way through the middle of the campus down to Lake Carnegie. We were like a couple of travelers from outer space, seeing buildings, grass and trees for the first time. And the winding sidewalks seemed to act like concrete funnels; we were being funneled somewhere. Perhaps we were going to be funneled into a human sized laboratory jar, with a label that said *homo sapiens mescalinensis*. And then they'd soak us in formaldehyde and leave us on a shelf in the biology lab. Abandon that thought—hurry, hurry, this could get scary. Our feet were walking normally, but it seemed that we were floating like ghosts down the walkways. We knew we were actually walking, but it sure seemed like we were hovering a few inches above the ground.

"Look at those tennis people," I whispered as we passed the tennis courts. People were playing tennis on several courts under the outdoor lighting.

"I see them. They seem to move faster than normal. Do you think they are? Or are we moving in slow motion? Why are we whispering?"

"I don't know. But I think we are moving in slow motion. I can hear them shout back and forth to one another. They seem to be moving in fast motion but talking in slow motion. I'm whispering because our voices might sound strange and I don't want anyone to get suspicious that we're on mescaline."

"Joey, that's so funny. No one would suspect that."

"Well, if they sound like they're talking in slow motion, then we must be talking faster than normal. And I think our arms and legs move like vampire or space alien arms. I've been glancing at both of our arms and legs while we're walking and they look very strange. What if people think we are from outer space and shoot us, like they did in that movie *The Day the Earth Stood Still?*"

"I loved that movie, Joey. Those people were not very nice to Klaatu, were they? But we have student I.D.'s. There are plenty of quirky people on this campus. No one would give us a second thought."

"Okay then, if we are stopped by campus police, I'll let you do the talking. No, you're liable to frighten them."

"What? I'll frighten them?"

"Yes, I've been watching you. You know I'm crazy about

your eyes. They are very beautiful. But now they are really dilated, like they're one big pupil. You will definitely be mistaken for someone from another planet. My friends say their pupils are dilated on LSD; I guess mescaline is the same. But yours look like giant observatory mirrors, or like they could shoot lasers out of them, like the robot in that movie."

"Oh, Gort, yes. Do I have robot eyes?"

"No, no, no. Your eyes are so gorgeous they make my knees buckle if I look at them too long. But now they look black instead of turquoise."

"Let me look at *your* eyes, Joey. That's what I thought; everyone's eyes look black in the dark."

As we were walking along Faculty Road we could see the headlight beam of a car approaching from behind us. I stopped in my tracks to stare at it as it passed by. I was sending it a stern visual message that I knew it was spying on us. "That car is spying on us, don't you think?"

"No one's spying on us, Joey. But I am not fond of these streetlights. Let's walk in the grass like we did Tuesday afternoon." She took my hand and we headed across the road toward the lake. Just then there was a sudden loud commotion by the water's edge.

"Yikes," I said.

"Wow," she said. "What was *that*?"

"It freaked me out; I'm still catching my breath. I thought it was a flying saucer at first. I think it was an owl. It grabbed a big rat or a muskrat. We'd better not put our blanket too close to the water."

"I'll say, but the lake looks magnificent. It's like a mirror. Let's hurry and get to our spot. It's not too much further."

We smelled the Lilac fragrance before spotting the tree. "Ahh, we're here," I said. "It smells stronger than it did before. Is that the mescaline talking, or is it more in bloom now? Where should we put the blanket?"

"Let's put it in the shadow of that tree over there. I don't want to see the streetlights," she said, while pointing to a good-sized tree, maybe one and a half stories tall, about a hundred feet further.

"That's good, because I think the Lilac is a little too sweet to smell for too long."

"I think the fragrance will be just right a little further away."

"If you wear lilac perfume, I'd say dilute it about fifty percent, and it would be just right."

"And then you would like it? I was thinking if I could find a perfume that smelled like your Nonna's spaghetti sauce..." Then she started laughing. We were talking while we walked along.

Then I started laughing. "Sure, but that would make me want to rush down to Camden for her spaghetti and meatballs. You'd get to meet my Nonna." I'm talking and laughing at the same time, laughing harder, which made it harder to get the words out.

"I look forward to meeting your Nonna." Mary's talking and laughing at the same time. "But I thought it would make you want to sprinkle some Parmesan on my neck and bite me like a Vampire." Now she was laughing so hard she had tears in her eyes and could hardly speak.

"No, it would have to be Pecorino-Romano, and I might want to lick it off your neck." Now I was laughing with tears in my eyes as well.

"That sounds nice, Joey." She turned serious for a moment. "You're making me forget what I came here for." Then she really started laughing and said, "Why don't you dip me in the sauce?"

Now my laugh turned into a nervous laugh, imagining *that*. I may have forgotten to mention that her passionate kiss in my car not too long ago was the first passionate kiss I ever had in my life. So now I'm practically shaking with fright at the same time that I am feeling a strange warm euphoria at the idea of licking Mary's body, with or without the sauce. "I can't dip you in it. It would be too hot. I'll have to let it cool off some, and then I could ladle it over you. What are we doing here anyway?"

Now she was getting nervous because I was nervous. The laughter stopped as quickly as it began. "I don't know. Let's just spread this blanket out to sit and watch the sky together. I want to look at the moon while we still can."

"That sounds good." We sat in the middle of the blanket. I was relieved. If we sat at either end of the blanket, then we would have room to stretch out and I would feel pressured to start making out. I had been looking forward to that with an equal mixture of enthusiasm and apprehension, because I had never made out before. I resolved to drink a few glasses of wine when the time came. On the mescaline I was extra nervous. I nudged closer to her, so that our shoulders were touching. She nudged even closer, so that our shoulders were practically melting into each other. I pointed to the moon.

"You can see the part that's in the earth's shadow with the binoculars," she said, as she reached into her tote bag for them.

"I'll look through them after you. Can you tell what kind of cheese it's made from with the binoculars? I don't know where I got that idea from."

"Huxley talked about the suchness or isness of objects. Did you read that part, Joey? The isness of the moon is overwhelming. It is so far away, yet it causes the tides on the earth. I was just eleven when they landed on the moon. It's a quarter million miles away."

"Not only that, but we're spinning, the moon is spinning and both orbits are elliptical. How did we ever aim the spacecraft accurately enough to land on it? That boggles the mind."

"Well, Joey, I bet you could figure it out. Here, try the binoculars."

"I don't think so. You're looking at someone who almost had a nervous breakdown trying to use a slide rule. Oh, I see it. I see it. These binoculars are way more powerful than the ones I used before. I could make out the craters before, but they were blurry. Now they are crystal clear."

"Most people can see blurry craters with the naked eye. Joey, you must be really nearsighted."

"I am. I'm supposed to wear my glasses when I drive, but I don't really wear them the rest of the time. I don't wear them to drive if I know the way. I have to wear them in classes, especially in the lecture halls, to see the blackboard. That's mainly the only time I wear them."

"Why don't you wear them to play pool, Joey? You would probably shoot better with them."

"I tried, but with my head down for the shot I'm looking through the frame instead of the lens. I shoot mostly by intuition. I can't explain it. Luckily I'm not trying to make a living at it."

"I shoot by intuition too. My eyes are never focused on the exact same spot."

"Then it's true what they say about a woman's intuition, because you're a much better shot than I am."

"Joey, let me see the binoculars, please. I want to look at the clouds." The sky was spotted with puffy clouds here and there, and some were now approaching the crescent moon. "I don't know if they are more beautiful in the moonlight or during the day."

"I think these clouds are as much illuminated by the town's lights as by the moon tonight."

"You're right, but they are illuminated. Now I see what Huxley meant about seeing the infinite in a single thing. Did you ever wonder how many drops of water are in a cloud? It strikes me in the same way as looking at a night sky full of stars. I don't care how many stars there actually are. I just wonder how far they go back, how far you can see into the universe. In stars, is it infinity? In clouds, you know they're finite, but they have the same inscrutability as a starry sky. I read this book called *The Cloud of Unknowing*. I found it in a used bookshop. It about how Catholic monks seeking God through contemplation come to a cloud—they say of unknowing, beyond which they can penetrate no further. So looking now through these binoculars at a physical cloud, whether in the moonlight, the streetlight, or the sunlight, I feel like God is in there, but just beyond my ability to see."

"I think your cloud of unknowing is clouding your view of the cloud in the here and now. The Catholic God is so anthropomorphic. Huxley was trying to see the unknowable God, your Ein Sof. Isn't it intrinsic to the cloud itself, not to something hidden in it?"

"That's true, Joey. The God that most Jews experience--and Christians, I might add--is anthropomorphic. Intellectually, I know the Ein Sof is neither he, she, nor it. Maybe it's all of those. In Kaufmann's *Critique*, he said that Judaism did not really define God, opening it up to all sorts of ideas. Like I said before, two Jews, three opinions. In my daily life I may see God as a kindly old grandfather figure. But I agree with you. I should try to focus on the cloud itself. I think it's going to hide the moon any minute."

"When I see clouds in moonlight, sometimes they remind me of those old Dutch paintings where the people wear dark outfits with these white collars."

"They're called ruffs."

"Oh, I never heard of that. But other times the light at the edge of the cloud is thinner, and very bright. It reminds me of a halo."

"I think I see a halo around you, Joey."

"Now you *are* hallucinating. But I am too. I read a book about Tibetan monks when I was young, and they could see people's auras. I see a gold aura around you. It's faint, but definitely gold. It's like an energy field. It looks like the heat waves you see off a hot pavement when driving in the middle of summer. Maybe you have a fever; let me feel your forehead. No, you're okay."

"I may be getting a fever, Joey, but not that kind."

I started laughing. At first it was a nervous laugh, from fear of making a fool of myself if that meant we were supposed to make out. But it morphed into a happy laugh, as it dawned on me that her feelings for me might have been just as strong as mine for her. Now she was laughing too. Why was she laughing? Did she guess that I was nervous about making out? Was she laughing at me? Or was she laughing with me, because we just had some cosmic connection and both realized that we were falling in love? How very unlikely it is that two people fall in love, and more unlikely that they do it at the same time, and even more unlikely that they do it at the same time and with the same intensity. So I found it hilarious that we could be so lucky, and I laughed all the harder.

But then I remembered all of Tiger's admonishing and

felt like I had to keep silent about it. I couldn't say, "I love you," or "I'm falling in love with you." That would put pressure on her to say the same, even if she didn't feel it. I stopped laughing. I knew that if I didn't start thinking about something else my laughter would turn to tears. I'm not a tearful person. The mescaline takes your emotions for a roller coaster ride. Here we are possibly in love, but we can't say a word about it. "The moon is behind the clouds. Can we see the stars now?" I turned around and stood up, more to hide a tear that I felt on my cheek than to see the stars.

She followed my lead and stood beside me. She started to raise the binoculars to her eyes but stopped short. "Joey, is that a tear? Are you sad?" Then she started to cry.

"No, it's a happy tear, probably from laughing too hard."

"Oh." Then she aimed the binoculars straight up. "I can see them; there are so many," she said. "I'm going to lie flat on the blanket so I won't get a sore neck. Lie next to me so we can share the binoculars."

"I hope I'll be able to see them, but I can't see them now," I said. I lay down next to her. Then I shimmied about a foot away from her. "I think we both need elbow room when we hold the binoculars up to our eyes."

Then she shimmied a little closer to me. "No, we don't, Joey. My elbows are above your shoulders when looking through them."

Now I started laughing. "Sure, but that's when you're looking through my shoulders. Or are you looking through your elbows? What happens when you're looking through the binoculars?"

"I am looking through the binoculars, silly. Oh, okay, you got me this time." Now she started laughing, which made me laugh harder, which started a chain reaction of laughter that was all out of proportion to the play on words.

"All right, let's be serious now," she said, as she handed the binoculars to me. "Look straight up with them, then tilt your head ever so slightly to the left." She was looking up with her naked eye to guide me. "There's a whole cluster of them, fading back into the distance. I can still make out the closer ones." Her head was tilted slightly to the left. I was on her right side.

"I see a star. I see it," I said. I had the binoculars trained directly at her. "It's beautiful. A beautiful movie star."

"A what?" she said as she turned toward me. "What are you doing, Joey?" Now she saw me aiming the binoculars at her.

"Just joking, I'll be serious now," I said. "But I'm not having the sort of experience that Huxley had. He was as uninterested in people—including his own wife, as he was intensely interested in the suchness of inanimate things. I'm just so intensely interested in the suchness, no, I should say the *you*-ness of *you*, that I find it hard to focus on anything else."

"I'm finding that you are quite a distraction as well. But I have only one chance to experience that *Mysterium Tremendum et Fascinans* I mentioned, so we need to try our best to focus."

"You're right, darling. But you should know that when I look at you, that is exactly what I experience. I feel like I can almost see deep inside your soul, maybe just to the point of that cloud of unknowing. You are mysterious and frightening. Not frightening, I mean you make me tremble. I don't believe in God. But you are so beautiful that I think a God had to create you. Here, you look at the stars," I said, handing her the binoculars. "I will lie here and look at you, but not directly. I can see you in my mind's eye, with my eyes closed."

"That's very sweet, Joey. I would like to stare into your soul too, but after my stargazing. Did you know that the universe is ten to twenty billion light years wide? And that it's expanding?" (That was the estimated size in 1977; now they think it's ninety-two billion light years.)

"Did Wheeler tell you that? Wilkinson said the same thing."

"Yes, but I've been reading more about it in the library as well."

"It doesn't make any sense to me. I grew up thinking the universe went on forever. Does the *space* that the universe occupies go on forever? Shouldn't it be infinite? If not, what happens if the universe runs out of room to expand?"

"I'm not concerned with that now. I just want to know who or what is behind it all. I know I can't see to the edge of the universe. But I want to look out at the stars and imagine how big it is."

"Well, ten to twenty billion light years doesn't sound too wide compared to infinity. How many miles wide is a light year?"

"Hah! It's crazy. Try around six trillion miles."

"One light year? Yikes."

"Yes, the universe is six trillion miles multiplied by ten or twenty billion."

"I can't fathom six trillion miles, let alone six trillion miles times one billion. And then times ten or twenty? So it's not infinitely wide, but still ridiculously wide. Huxley focused more on the intensity of experience, and not quantities. So the universe's size shouldn't matter."

"I know, and I was thinking maybe I bit off more than I can chew. Maybe it's impossible to experience the suchness or isness of something as vast as the universe. But I want to lie here quietly for a while and try."

"I'll be very quiet."

"Joey, I'm getting chilly. Would you hand me my jacket out of the tote bag, please?"

"Sure. I think I need mine too."

We lay there for what seemed like several hours. I confess that I probably don't have the attention span to appreciate the mescaline experience. I tried looking at the folds of my jacket sleeve, I tried lying on my stomach to stare at blades of grass and even at the dirt. I looked at the water. I kept getting drawn back to Mary. In my mind's eye I could see her turquoise eyes framed by that red hair, her very fair skin, her soft, downy, reddish blond eyebrows —she didn't pluck them. Her long legs seemed to go on forever, although hidden under an olive-green, bell bottom, khaki jumpsuit. How would I see into her soul? In her there had to be a soul, or a spirit at least. Even if there was no God, there was something numinous about her. Maybe I was lying here next to a goddess. Now I opened my eyes and turned toward her. I wondered whether to fix my gaze at her head or at her heart. Philosophers through the ages have debated the location of the soul, from Aristotle with the heart, to Descartes with the pineal gland at the base of the brain. I settled on the brain, because I've always believed that the mind is located there. And if there is a soul, then it must be located in the mind. So while she looked up at the stars, I stared into her ear. Her ears attached to her head without an earlobe hanging down, whereas mine had pronounced earlobes. Her ears were much smaller than mine, and very pretty. She wore a small gold earring with an opal stone. I could barely make it out in the dark. But when we got back to my dorm I was mesmerized by it. It was not her birthstone, but it had mysterious qualities that made it especially appropriate for that night. I could barely see the closest stars looking at the sky, but back in the dorm I felt that I could see the whole universe in her opal. Here in the dark, on the blanket by the lake, I tried to see through her ear and peer into her innermost mental chambers to see her soul.

Then suddenly I felt like I was doing it all wrong. I always imagined that the soul had the exact shape as our physical body. So maybe I should be looking in the vicinity of her center of gravity, her navel. Now I thought I should be navel gazing in every sense of the word, except at Mary's navel. I was just switching my attention in that direction when she turned and nudged me with her hand. "Joey, it's too cloudy now. We should head back to your dorm."

"Oh, okay. But I must tell you that I've been peering into your soul."

"What did you see? Anything?"

"Anything? I wouldn't call that just anything. Your soul looked like Joan of Arc, or Guinevere, or some Greek or Roman Goddess on a big white horse, except it was you. You were holding a sword in one hand, and a shield as well as the horse reins in the other hand. You had just broken through the gates of heaven, and you were there to demand that God tell you the truth about the universe and about him."

"What did he say?"

"I don't know. You just nudged me out of it."

"Do you want to stay here a little longer and try to see what happens next?"

"No, to be honest, I don't know if it was really your soul. I tried my hardest to look at things intensely, like Huxley did. But my malfunctioning brain wouldn't let me. It started inventing stories about everything I tried to look at."

"I'm ready for a glass of that Chianti. Did you get any soda?" She said, as she stood up.

I stood up and helped her fold the blanket. "I bought a small bottle of 7-UP. Did you see the *Mysterium* thing?"

"It wasn't as profound as Huxley's. I was trying to experience the vastness of the universe. I guess I wouldn't sense the All in an object, if my object of observation was the All in itself. But I did feel a sense of its vastness more deeply than I think I would have otherwise, and a sense that God has a lot more on his plate than I thought before. He's in charge of ten or twenty billion multiplied by six trillion miles worth of universe. What time is it?"

I looked at my watch. "It's one o'clock."

"Oh my goodness, we've been here since about nine o'clock. That's four hours."

We walked back through the campus to my dorm. At first we tried to walk arm in arm, which felt awkward-- because I'm such a klutz or was it the mescaline? So we switched to holding hands. We saw a campus police car with its headlights on, parked behind Dillon Gym. Besides that, there wasn't a soul stirring.

We bounded up the three flights of stairs effortlessly, almost like we floated up, which told me that the effects of the mescaline were nowhere close to wearing off.

"I have a corkscrew around here somewhere," I said, as I fumbled in my desk drawers looking for it. "Ahh, I found it." I poured us each a glass of wine, and then added a splash of 7-UP from the fridge. Tiger's father bought him a compact refrigerator, which he shared with me.

Mary was looking through our record albums, an eclectic mix. "Can I hear 'Rhapsody in Blue?' Father loves that song."

"Sure you can. We can't play it too loud. I don't know

how many other students are still around. I don't want to wake up anyone. I'll put it on for you. Tiger has one of those expensive direct drive turntables. He's very fussy about it."

"Pure genius that Gershwin," she said as she sipped her wine while listening.

"That's Tiger's record. He loves the old Big Band sound, Glenn Miller and all of that. But I do love that opening clarinet."

"Father is especially fond of Jewish composers, George Gershwin of course, Aaron Copland, Felix Mendelssohn. He's not too fond of Phillip Glass."

"How about César Franck? I have his Violin Sonata. Isn't he Jewish?"

"I love that sonata, but he's not Jewish. I think he's French or Dutch."

"But Anne Frank is Jewish. Isn't Franck also a Jewish name?"

"They have different spellings. I'm pretty sure he's not Jewish. Father likes that sonata; he would have told me if Franck was Jewish. He wanted me to be proud that I'm Jewish. Now I want to hear something on this Jimi Hendrix album. Oh, this is perfect. How about 'Hey Joe'?"

"But he shot his old lady. I'm not like that. Am I? If you were 'messing around with another man,' I think I'd just walk away. No, I'd *run* away. No, I'd, I don't know. I'd be sad, I think. What if we play 'Foxy Lady' instead?"

"I have an idea. Let's listen to his 'Star-Spangled Banner.'"

"That sounds good, but it's on the *Woodstock* Album. We have it in there somewhere." I put on the song and turned the volume up a tiny bit. "He's beyond brilliant, isn't he?"

"I'll say, way beyond. Hendrix is a god. What a senseless loss."

We listened to it a few times, nodding to each other throughout the song. The human face is capable of so many expressions. We found dozens of them between the two of us to say, in complete silence, "Pure genius, I couldn't agree more, that is divine, a god for sure, I'm with that, yes, I dig it, this blows my mind, don't you know it, Yikes, Wow, etc." It was like we both had a direct encounter with the *musical* version of the *Mysterium Tremendum et Fascinans*.

We were sitting on a small sofa—really a loveseat—that was left in our dorm room by the previous occupants. Now I became mesmerized by her opal earrings. "Have you ever stared at your earrings, I mean just one of them?"

"Of course I have. Girls generally look at earrings carefully before purchasing them. We want to know not just how they look, but we'll ponder how they'll look with this hat or that outfit. Do they flatter my eyes? Are they too big for my ears? All that sort of stuff."

"But I'm talking about the universe. When I stare at your opal, I can see far into the universe. I see galaxies and nebulae."

"You do? Let me take one of them off so I can see too. Oh, I do; I see nebulae. They say you can see the Orion Nebula in the night sky with the naked eye, but I never looked for it."

Before Mary could suggest another record, I asked for her help. "You know these books that Professor Kaufmann gave me? That Nietzsche is very hard to follow. I tried to read his *Genealogy of Morals* and it's very confusing. You said earlier that you read it. Maybe you can help me, not tonight, but later maybe?"

"He's not easy to read. It's very helpful to read

Kaufmann's preface and introduction before you start on the actual book."

"Oh, I always skip them. Let me try reading that. Should I put on another record?" I said as I walked over to our bookcase to get the Nietzsche book.

"No, thanks. I'm enjoying the quiet."

"Do you mind if I look at Kaufmann's introduction? Or we could do anything you like. Do you want to look at our chair legs, or at the folds in our army blanket draperies?"

"You can read Kaufmann's intro if you like. I want to watch a spider web that I noticed under your amplifier. But first I have to go to the ladies' room."

"The ladies' room is up the hall on your left. It's right after the men's room. I'll come with you, I mean to the men's room. I have to pee. Remind me to get rid of that spider web when we get back."

"No, don't you dare. I want to study it."

I waited in the hall for her to come out of the ladies room. When we got back to the room Mary asked if she could use my desk lamp to look at the spider web.

"I'll unplug it for you. The plug is behind my desk. I'll have to slide it out a little."

"I can plug it in over here," she said. "I see the extension cord under the table."

Like most dorm rooms, around the stereo especially, ours was a tangle of extension cords and speaker wires. My desk lamp was the kind with the flexible neck that Mary could twist to aim right into the spider web.

"It's shaped like a teeny tiny horn of plenty. I can see him deep inside there."

"I think it's a she. Most webs are spun by the females. We used to see them in the summers when I was in elementary school. Tap the outside of the web very lightly and the spider will come out. She'll think it's an insect for dinner. Here, here's a pencil."

"I don't want to disturb him, I mean her. I just want to look."

"All right sweetheart, I'm going to just glance through Kaufmann's intro to see if it helps."

"If you're going to call me sweetheart, then I'm going to call you sweetie. That's what Mother calls Father. Father calls her pumpkin."

"Do you want me to call you pumpkin?"

"No. I think it's weird. I know a lot of men call their wives pumpkin. But it seems like a very odd term of endearment."

"Maybe it's because it's a dessert. Something sweet."

"Yes, but not to the point, like sweetie or sweetheart. And they both call each other honey sometimes."

"I'll call you sweetheart. I like sweetheart. I like honey too. But sometimes darling will slip right out for no reason."

"Okay, then I'll call you sweetie or honey, unless dear happens to slip right out for no reason."

"I like that."

"Me too, sweetie."

"Okay, darling, now I'll see what Kaufmann has to say." With that we both started laughing. "I can't believe we are saying all this darling, sweetie, honey sweetheart stuff. I'm really happy about it, but it's very funny at the same time. Do you think we would say all that if we weren't on mescaline?"

"No, dear, we'd be afraid." She started laughing as she got the words out, which started me laughing, which made her laugh more.

I managed to say, while laughing so uncontrollably that I could barely speak, "Is this one of those feedback loops you told me about in chaos theory? I say sweetheart, you say dear, I say darling, you say honey."

With that she stopped laughing. "I hope you feel the same about me tomorrow, without the mescaline," she said.

"I felt this way long before we did the mescaline. You got nothing to worry about...*honey*."

"That's very sweet, Joey."

I turned on the pole lamp by the sofa and sat down to read. Mary went back to observing her spider web. We spent almost two more hours in these pursuits. It was nearly four o'clock in the morning.

"I got it. I got it."

"What, sweetie? Did Kaufmann's intro help you?"

"Yes, but I meant my senior thesis topic."

"You have your thesis topic? That's great. What is it?"

"That Nietzsche makes perfect sense if the reader is on mescaline."

"Will you need to take more mescaline?"

"I don't see the need for more mescaline. I just have to show that mescaline *expands* the mind of a sober, sane, intelligent person, making him for a few hours at least, more like a mad genius than he would be otherwise. I can rely solely on Huxley for that—the *argumentum ad verecundiam*, the appeal to authority. He said it, and he took the mescaline. Who's going to argue with that? The point is that Nietzsche is clearly a mad genius, and someone in the same state, albeit an altered state, can much better understand him."

"Are you going to ask Professor Kaufmann to be your thesis advisor? He'll want you to read a lot more of Nietzsche."

"Then I will have to take more mescaline."

"Kaufmann has so many commentaries and

introductions to his Nietzsche translations that can help you. Maybe if you read those thoroughly you won't need more mescaline."

"But if I can understand him without taking more mescaline, then I don't have a thesis."

"Sounds like a catch 22. Nietzsche said that you have to read his books in chronological order—forwards and backwards, and then you have to ruminate on them, if you want to understand them. So to understand him, you almost have to become a Nietzsche scholar. That said, I wouldn't mind doing mescaline again later this summer."

"Mine's starting to wear off now."

"Mine is too. I think I'm ready to have some wine and try to sleep."

I poured us some wine and we sat together on the sofa. After a couple more glasses the bottle was finished and my IQ dropped about fifty points. After a bumbling attempt to kiss her on the lips, I leaned back and said, "Do you believe in love at first sight?"

"Well, dear Joey, I have seriously fallen for you, but I can't say exactly when it happened."

"I've been scared to death to say it up until now, but I love you. I love you madly. Tiger warned me that guys think they're in a relationship when they're actually the only one in it. I can just imagine how stupid he'll think I am for coming right out and saying I love you."

"That's not stupid. That's honest. At least if the girl didn't have the same feelings for you, then you would know sooner. But I do; I love you too." With that she pulled me in for another kiss.

"Well then, Tiger will think *you're* stupid too. What do you see in me? I'm skinny as a toothpick, I'm very clumsy and I have a big nose. I'm not a jock, I'm not very smart and I'm definitely not rich."

"Stop it, Joey. Remember that I asked you to join me for tea the moment I met you. You talk about my eyes, but I saw something in you that attracted me. You could have been a campus carpenter with a nail apron on and I would have invited you for tea just the same. I can't say that I looked into your eyes and saw your soul. But I saw your suchness, your isness, or as you call it, your you-ness, and I was quite drawn to it."

"Then do you think we should get married?"

"When Father asked Mother, she told him, 'I think we should sleep on it,' so that's my answer too. Would you mind standing over by the window seat and looking the other way? I want to change into my pajamas."

"Sure, and then you look the other way, so I can change into my gym shorts. I sleep in gym shorts and a tee shirt. And then I'll get Tiger's bed ready for you. I have some clean linens for it."

"We're both a little wobbly from the wine, sweetie. Let me help you get the bed ready."

"Do you like to sleep in pitch dark, or with a light?"

"Maybe a tiny bit of light, do you have a nightlight?"

"I can leave the army blanket drape drawn a little, so the outside lights will be a nightlight." With that I gave her one last kiss, a goodnight kiss, and we crawled under our blankets.

After a minute or so, Mary sat up and reminded me that it would be daylight soon. "Maybe we can put the desk light under the end table on the other side of the sofa. It won't be too bright, but it will keep us from tripping over something when we get up."

I got up, moved the lamp, and then closed the army-blanket drape all the way. I was almost asleep when I felt Mary climbing into my bed. "I'll sleep better if you just hug me," she said as she turned away from me, pulling my arm over her as she turned. We slept that way until late in the afternoon.

When I awoke, she had already showered and dressed. She was lying next to me and staring at the ceiling. I wasn't sure, but I thought that we might have done something really serious sometime in our sleep. It would have been my first time for sure. I reached under the covers with one hand to surreptitiously check that I still had my gym shorts on. "Did we? No, we couldn't have. I didn't try anything in my sleep, did I? Maybe it was a dream. Did anything happen last night?"

"I don't remember anything happening. We slept straight through. On the question of marriage, after sleeping on it, I'd say if we're going to get married, first you would have to ask Father's permission, and then you would have to propose. Father will pull Mother aside and ask her to pull me aside to ask me if I'm pregnant. She will also want to reassure him that I am still a virgin. Of course I will tell her that I'm still a virgin. I could never lie to Mother. So you see, dear, nothing could have happened. Maybe you had a dream."

"Then it was a very sweet dream, the sweetest dream I ever had. I think I need to have a talk with your father."

"Mother is picking me up Tuesday morning. Wednesday we fly to Saint Augustine to spend ten days at Aunt Edna's. You can come to dinner at our house after we return. Mother already knows all about you."

"Yikes. What did you tell her?"

"I told her you were clumsy, but in a lovable way like Dick Van Dyke, that you were chivalrous, but not a male chauvinist, that your mind was as unruly as your hair, but capable of brilliant lightning-bolt insights, like Kaufmann said of Nietzsche, and that you were sweet and kind; but most importantly, for reasons I can't explain, that I adored you and that it seemed like you obviously adored me. She was most intrigued to hear that you were a skilled carpenter. I said don't get any ideas, Mother."

"Don't tell her that. For *your* mother, I'd do anything in the world."

The Malin Family Episode

Human earnestness, so fearfully direct, so anxious to improve, builds monuments to house the living God and kills him dead within an ornamental prison.

— Eric Graham Howe

I HAD A FULL SUMMER'S WORTH OF CARPENTRY projects in Princeton to keep me busy. The most interesting one was a two-story, detached, single car garage I would build for a lady in town. It was modeled on a barn she saw on a trip through Pennsylvania Dutch Country, with board and batten siding painted red, as well as a five foot diameter painted *barn star/hex sign* in the shape of a twelve-pointed rose *compass* that would be centered on the gable. The most boring one was spending ten hours a week for the entire summer adjusting door closers for the university carpentry shop. Working ten hours a week on campus entitled me to dormitory housing for the summer. The previous two summers I went home and worked with my father on his projects. But home was forty miles south of Princeton and

Mary lived around sixty miles north. To see her I would have had to drive a hundred miles each way. So adjusting door closers for ten hours a week in order to live on campus made sense.

Nowadays door closers are more compact. But back in 1977 they were shaped like an upside down bell that was four to five inches in diameter but weighed as much as the Liberty Bell. They were filled with hydraulic fluid. There were several adjustments. The *sweep speed* valve controlled how fast the door closed overall. The *delayed action* valve controlled how fast the door closed in the initial half of the sweep. The *latch speed* valve controlled how fast the door closed just before it latched. And still another, the *back check* valve, controlled how fast the door opened, so that it would not fly open on a windy day. These adjustments would not be so complicated were they all independent. But they were *interdependent*: adjusting one required you to go back to the previous one and readjust it. Sometimes one of them just wouldn't work right no matter what I tried. Then I had to ask one of the senior carpenters to look at it. If he couldn't adjust it, then I would replace it with a new one. Adjusting them was the carpenter's version of my older cousin Nick adjusting his twin carburetors on his old MG Midget, which he had to do almost every time he drove it. In my teens I got to watch him slam the hood and throw his wrench into the woods behind his house on several occasions. His mom, my aunt Isabelle, had a large, finished basement where we had many of our family gatherings—for holidays, weddings, funerals, birthdays, and my favorite, the Christmas Eve Feast of the Seven Fishes.

The university let students who were staying on for the summer remain in their old dorms until whatever dormitory would serve as summer housing was ready for them. That summer it was Spelman Hall, where four students shared a four-bedroom apartment with a kitchen. During the school year it housed students who preferred to do their own cooking. During the summer the dining halls were closed, so it was useful to have a kitchen. Along with my personal belongings, I had to move Tiger's fridge, the stereo and the loveseat with me to Spelman. This would be after commencement and the reunion crowds left the campus.

In the summer of 1977 cell phones were almost as expensive as a new car and extremely rare. Answering machines were still a rarity. So it helped to plan ahead if you wanted to reach someone by phone. We planned for me to call Mary at nine AM on Friday, and Mary would call me at nine AM the following Wednesday, the day before they flew back home.

"Guess what?" she said when she called. "Mother invited you for dinner at our house on Sunday."

"Yikes. That's quick."

"Did you get cold feet, Joey?"

"No. Just the opposite. I'd marry you tomorrow if I could. I'm not sure what I should wear to meet your parents. I have a black suit at home I wore last year to my Uncle Pete's funeral, but it's at home. I could drive home Saturday to get it. Can I wear my desert boots with it? I have a pair of Hush Puppies and work boots. Maybe I should wear my Hush Puppies; they're a darker brown. I have sandals but they hurt my toes."

"Stop it, sweetie. We're not getting married Sunday. Just wear anything that you would wear to a class. If I had to pick something out for you, I would say wear your bellbottom jeans with a knit shirt and any shoes you want. You should wear something comfortable for playing pool. I'm sure that Father would enjoy a game of pool."

"If I'm asking for your father's permission to marry you, shouldn't I wear a suit? I can wear my fedora with it. Should I wear my fedora?"

"Absolutely not. You'll look more Jewish than Father. I know what will look nice. Wear your khakis with the Princeton Sailing Club shirt—very preppy."

"But I'm not in the sailing club anymore."

"If he asks, then tell him you used to be. He's not going to give you the third degree about your shirt."

"I'd better rehearse what I'll say. I always rehearse with Tiger. I'm getting nervous just thinking about it. I have Tiger's number in Hong Kong. It's an expensive call, but I better call him."

"Don't call Tiger, honey. You don't have to rehearse. You're supposed to be nervous in that situation. Father would be suspicious if you weren't nervous. Mother and I already talked about this. By the way, we have her blessing. I invited you to our house for a Sunday afternoon game of straight pool, and Mother chimed in, 'Why don't you ask him to stay for dinner?' When you arrive, I will tell Father that I hope he can join us for a three-way game, which he will most certainly do, because he won't be too thrilled about you and me in the basement alone. You and Father are closely matched in skill. Then during the game, I will ask for a pause to go to the powder room. You and Father will have to wait for me to return, and that's when you can ask him."

"What if he starts yelling and screaming? Should I just leave? What should I do?"

"Father isn't the type to yell and scream. If he says no, Mother and I will gang up on him. Listen, I have to go. Call me Sunday morning around ten o'clock and I'll give you directions to our house. Hey, Joey."

"What?"

"I miss you."

"I miss you too."

I spent that Saturday afternoon at my parents' house and got them to help me rehearse. My dad told me how he asked Pop-Pop, my mom's dad, for permission. (We called my mom's dad Pop-Pop and my dad's dad Nonno. Don't ask me why. We called my dad's mom Nonna and my mom's mom Nonnina. Nonnina means little grandmother, and mom's mom was short, barely five feet tall.) Pop-Pop just wanted to know how many kids my dad wanted. Dad gave the right answer, at least a half dozen. Sadly for Pop-Pop, my mom had only one child. I have that in common with Mary. Neither of us has siblings. I would have loved to have a brother or sister, or a half a dozen brothers and sisters. My mom gave me my great-grandmother's engagement ring.

"Mom, I don't know if or when I'll be able to use it."

"What are you talking about? Hang on to it just in case. What's not to like about you? Of course you'll use it."

"Mom, her dad might think she should marry a Jew."

Then my dad chimed in, "It's all the same, Joey. We got the exact same nose. Italians and Jews were marrying since the Roman times. I worked with this stone mason on the addition to Our Lady of Mount Carmel, Benny Luzzato, Italian looking, Italian sounding as it gets. Big Italian nose like mine. Wore a fedora all the time. One day an elderly nun walks by and says the stonework is beautiful. Benny takes his hat off and bows graciously, saying Grazie Mille. He's wearing one of those Jewish beanie hats under his fedora."

"It's called a yarmulke, dad."

"What do *I* know. I don't know *nothing*. Go figure. But he was an Italian Jew, or really an Italian-American Jew. Or he was a Jewish-Italian-American. Like I said, I don't know *nothing*."

I called Mary Sunday morning for directions and last minute planning. "My dad thinks we should get married. He says Italians and Jews have the same nose because we intermarried since the Roman times."

"Your father sounds nice. Joey. I can't wait to meet him."

"You'll love my dad. But why is your nose small and straight like a movie star's? Did your ancestors intermarry with movie stars?"

"Very funny, sweetie. I take after Mother. She has red hair and a nose like mine. There may be some Nordic genes on her side."

I may have said somewhere that I am easily distracted. I don't remember what I was thinking about, but I missed my turnpike exit, and had to go to the next one and turn around. I might have saved time by reversing direction at the rest stop, but I wasn't sure that I could do that. In south Jersey, the toll-free I-295 runs parallel and close to the turnpike, so we rarely used the turnpike.

Mary's house was a split level with a two-car garage. The street sloped, so a split level was a good choice for the sloped lot. There was a curved sidewalk leading from the driveway to the porch stairs. The sidewalk was bordered with creeping juniper along both sides, and there were blue, purple and pink hydrangeas along the front of the house. There was a Volvo station wagon in the driveway. First I pulled up alongside it. I got out of my car and then I got back in. I hoped no one was watching. I thought I'd better park on the street in case another car was in the garage on my side and they had to use it to go to the store or something.

"Mother saw you out the kitchen window and thought you were leaving."

"I was afraid someone might need to pull in or out of the garage door on that side."

"He's very considerate, Mother. This is Joey. Joey, this is my mother, Hannah."

"So pleased to meet you, Joey."

"Very happy to meet you, er, shouldn't I call you Mrs. Malin, er, Doctor Malin or Professor Malin?"

"Hannah's fine. It makes me feel younger."

"Father took the dog out back. He'll be in shortly."

"Will Mr. Malin, er, the *other* Doctor Malin like me to call you by your first name? I don't know what he'll think of me. Can I call you Doctor Hannah? It sounds more respectful."

"I think that works, Mother. Surely Father doesn't think Joey should call both of you Doctor Malin. How will you know to whom he's speaking at the dinner table? It's the perfect solution."

"Doctor Hannah, I am sorry to hear that Darwin passed away."

"That's very kind of you, Joey. He was in our family for so long. We were all very sad for a long time. It was about five years ago. Just wait until you meet Moses, his successor. Joachim will be in with him any minute."

"I must ask, Doctor Hannah, how did you go from having a dog named Darwin to one named Moses?"

"Mother let me tell him, please? It was so funny, Joey. Father said it was his turn to name the dog, since Mother chose Darwin's name. Getting Darwin was Mother's idea; Father had no strong feelings one way or another about getting a dog. But when we decided to get Moses, Father said that as an observant Jewish man, he felt uncomfortable all those years when introducing Darwin to his friends. Now he is proud to introduce them to Moses."

"Well, I look forward to meeting Moses, who no doubt is named after as illustrious a figure as Darwin."

"True, but he's only half as illustrious in *size* as Darwin," Doctor Hannah said. "Darwin was a standard poodle. Moses is a miniature poodle. With Mary off to college and our getting older, Moses is easier to care for."

As she spoke a little grey poodle came running up the two half-flights of stairs, from the family room to the foyer level, then to the main living level where we were standing. His tail was wagging happily as he jumped up and down right in front of me, but without jumping on me. Well-trained, I thought. He was joyfully squealing in anticipation of making my acquaintance. I kneeled down to his size so I could shake his hand, pat his back, rub his head behind his ears, and all the formalities that *some* dogs expect upon first meeting someone. Moses was clearly the sort of dog who delighted in meeting new people.

Next, I didn't get quite as warm a welcome from her father, but he was very cordial. Mary said, "Father, this is my boyfriend Joey."

"Yes, pleased to meet you. Mary told me a little about you; you're a psychology major."

I interrupted, "I hope she told you theoretical, er, *cognitive* psychology, not clinical. Nice to meet you, Doctor Malin."

"But they're related, aren't they? They inform one another, I'm sure."

"That's a good point, sir. I haven't thought about that. But yes, I should be interested in the clinical side where it informs our understanding of how we think, er, cognition."

"I am much farther removed from clinical psychology than you. Joey. But..."

"Father, forgive me for interrupting, but why don't you and Joey continue this discussion downstairs. Please join us in a game of three-way straight pool."

"Oh, that's right. You said he was a decent pool player. All right Joey, let's see how good you are."

"I'm not consistent, Doctor Malin. I'll make a hard shot and then I'll miss an easy one. I'm really bad at setting up break shots. Oh, wait. Mary says you have a twelve foot snooker table. I'm nearsighted. Prepare to be very unimpressed with my playing." With that Mary took charge of directing us down to the basement, in a succession of three half-flights of stairs. Moses rushed through a zigzag obstacle course of six different legs as though he had to get out in front to part the Red Sea for us. What he really wanted was to take the center position on the old but comfy looking leather couch that was on a raised platform that overlooked the pool table.

"He doesn't have the slightest interest in the game. But he's very smart, and chose that spot because it's where he'll be most likely to have a warm body next to him," Mary said.

"Yes, and it's usually mine when I play against Mary," Doctor Malin said.

"I'm sure it will be mine, playing against the two of you," I said.

This time we flipped a coin for the break, three coins actually. If all three coins land on the same side, then you flip again until there's an odd man out. That person can choose to break or to shoot second or third. Then the other two flip just one coin. One person flips it and the other calls heads or tails. Doctor Malin lost and had to break. Mary chose the third spot, so that left me to shoot second.

Doctor Malin played a textbook *safe*. For a safe on the opening break, two balls have to hit a cushion after the cue ball makes contact with the rack. He played it beautifully, leaving the cue ball at the far end of the table, with the two balls on the far corners of the rack barely out enough from the rack, after bouncing off the cushions and back to the rack, for the next player to try a bank shot, which, owing to the nuances of a table on which I have never played before, I promptly missed. He and I both knew what would follow, and we took our places on either side of Moses, while Mary ran several racks. (Mary's cue stick was a Meucci. I know what some of my worldly-wise readers are thinking, because I was thinking the exact same thing. That proves it: Mary and I are soulmates.)

"So you were saying, Doctor Malin, that you were far removed from clinical psychology. Mary told me you were a theologian at Columbia, specializing in Judaism."

"That's right, I'm pretty far removed. But I'm working with a colleague, a clinical psychology professor, on a paper about the psychological traits of God that can be gleaned from the Jewish scripture, and how those may have changed over time—not over God's time, but over the time period in the Torah."

"Sounds interesting. What sort of traits?"

"On the good side, for example, is he caring, generous, kind, fair, patient, principled, selfless, and so forth? On the bad side, is he domineering, mean, short tempered, impatient, narcissistic, and so on? And in today's jargon, is he a control freak? And does he change over time--does he exhibit more or less of a given trait over time? Does he mellow out, or does he become a cranky old man? And looking at all of this as a scholar, can we really say this or that is exactly what God said or did, or were the writers projecting their own personality traits onto God? So there's a lot to research here. My expertise is in parsing God's exact words or deeds--through the various translations and using the commentaries in the Talmud, so that my colleague can scrutinize them for various psychological traits."

"Mary, it sounds like your father's paper may overlap your senior thesis. Have you been listening to our conversation?"

"I'm sorry, Joey, I'm so focused on my shots that I really couldn't say whether you were talking about cars, or sports, or philosophy."

"Mary knows about my research, and we've discussed her idea for her senior thesis. We have very little overlap. She's going to look at the metaphysical nature of God from the viewpoints of all that's been written about him by a wide selection of religious and non-religious thinkers. I'm looking at the personality traits of a strictly Jewish God, from strictly Jewish writings."

"Father is right. I told him I don't want to read his paper or discuss it anymore until I am finished with my thesis. If I use any of it in my thesis, then I would have to cite my own father's work, which feels uncomfortable. I discussed it with Professor Kaufmann, and he agrees it's best if I don't read Father's paper for my thesis."

Their basement was large and clean, but it was not like some that are finished into a recreation room, a *rec* room everyone called it. Their ceiling had exposed floor joists, with visible pipes and wires running through them. The concrete floor was painted a glossy grey and the exposed masonry walls were a flat white. In one corner there was a laundry area, with a washer, a dryer, a laundry sink, and one of those indoor clothes lines about six feet by six feet that folded like an umbrella and sat on a foldable tripod. It had cords about four inches apart. It probably held a lot of clothes. But it was not in use now, as the weather was perfect this time of year for hanging clothes outside to dry. Another corner had a round, dark-stained, wood card table, a large one that had six chairs around it, but looked like it could hold eight. One whole wall was lined with closets, with four pairs of varnished lauan veneer, bifold doors.

"Doctor Malin, most basements have more support columns. I see you have a heavy duty steel beam over the snooker table."

"Yes, I had the builder do that to eliminate the middle column, so I would have room to play. For a six by twelve foot table you need about eighteen by twenty-four feet clear, by the time you add another five foot average for the cue sticks, plus a foot for swinging the stick to shoot. I wanted a clear six feet all around the table."

Mary sunk forty-seven balls in a row before missing a long bank shot. Now it was her father's turn. "Excuse me for a few minutes; I have to go to the powder room. Go ahead and take your turns while I'm gone," Mary said.

Uh oh. That was my signal to ask the big question. Her father was walking around the table to choose a shot. I was visibly shaking as I interrupted him, and although I'm not generally a stutterer, I stuttered, "Doctor Malin, could we ah, ah, stop a minute?"

"Sure, what's the matter, Joey? Are you okay? Do you need the restroom too? There's another one on the second floor? Hannah will show you."

"No, sir, I mean yes, sir. Doctor, er, Doctor Malin, ahem, I need to ask you, er, or should I get on my knees and beg you, um, I am asking for your permission to marry your daughter. Whew. I can't believe I said it. But yes, I am in love with Mary and I believe she loves me too. . ."

"Joey, let me stop you right there. You seem like a very nice young man. I was very concerned when Mary told us she was dating a gentile. But her mother said not to worry. Mary's had a few other boyfriends in high school and college, and she eventually decided they weren't for her. But you're the first *gentile* she's dated. Hannah said, 'She'll probably tire of him like she did with the others; don't make a big thing out of it.' But I see she fooled us this time. It's not personal. But people have been trying to destroy the Jewish race for centuries. I'm just strongly against diluting the Jewish race."

Now I should have told him what my dad said about Italians and Jews marrying since Roman times, but I couldn't speak. My tongue was glued to its surroundings from the worst case of dry mouth I ever had. It was like a severe case of stage fright. Not that I've ever been on a stage; just the thought of it gives me stage fright. Fortunately we were interrupted by Mary coming down the stairs, along with her mother, who carried a tray with a tea kettle, cups, cookies and all the necessities for afternoon teatime. "I thought everyone might like some tea," her mother said, as she set the tray down on the card table.

Her father was a little nervous now, as he got straight to the point. "Hannah, Joey just asked my permission to marry our daughter."

"Well, I'm so happy for them. Mazel Tov, congratulations."

"You know how I feel; I've told you."

Mary motioned me over to the card table in the corner. "Will you have some tea, Joey? I could make you some coffee if you prefer."

I was still struggling to get my tongue unstuck from the rest of my mouth. So I shook my head yes to the tea and no to the coffee. I needed to get some liquid in there quick. She poured us each a cup of tea. I put some cream and a teaspoon of sugar in mine and took a few small sips. Now I could open my mouth, but Mary whispered, "Let Mother handle this."

"I understand your feelings, Joachim, but can I share a paleontologist's perspective?"

"We're not talking about dinosaurs, Hannah. We're talking about centuries, no thousands of years of people trying to wipe out the Jews. By marrying gentiles, we will eventually wipe *ourselves* off the planet, without a single shot being fired."

"I'm not talking about dinosaurs. I'm talking about *all* species, past and present. Well, not all. But in every species that has been studied, *except* for humans, the *rare* individual—we've talked about genotypes and phenotypes before--the albino, or any different color for that matter, the rare hair or eye color, the different plumage, and the individual from a different variety, or race, if you will, has an advantage in mating. All species are genetically programmed by natural selection to want to expand and mix their gene pool as much as possible, to avoid the deleterious effects of inbreeding. Humans have perverted this evolutionary advantage into its polar opposite, so that we are segregated into separate races, ethnicities, religions, and even the various sects of any given religion. As someone whose life work is to study evolution, I think that humanity would greatly benefit from diluting not just the Jewish race, but *all* races, religions and ethnicities. If we were in a *real* melting pot, and it was allowed to reach its logical conclusion, then maybe there would be no more wars, wars caused by our racism, xenophobia, jingoism, sectarianism, and so on."

"Let's not argue, Hannah. Not many kids these days ask for the father's permission to marry. I should be thankful for that." He looked over at me. "Joey, this is nothing against you. I can't tell her who to marry. Mary is an adult now. But I cannot in good conscience give *my* blessing for her marry a gentile. As her father, it's been my dream, practically since Mary was born, to have a big Jewish wedding for her someday, and then Jewish grandchildren, the boys wearing their little yarmulkes, taking all the grandchildren to the Big Sea Day parade in Point Pleasant, where we've taken Mary many times—stopping in at the Abromowitz Department Store to buy them something nice. And besides all that, I will have contributed to the preservation of Judaism."

"We could raise our children Jewish. Would that help? They can wear yarmulkes," I said.

"My turn now, Father," Mary said. "I'm in love with Joseph. I didn't set out to fall in love with a Catholic, or a Jew, or an agnostic for that matter. Joey and I were exiting the library at the same time. We were both instantly attracted to each other. It's kismet, fate, or destiny, whatever you want to call it. I invited him to have some tea. I did not wake up that morning and say, 'I think I'll fall in love today.' Or do you think a Dybbuk put the idea in my head, or was it an angel?"

"What's a Dybbuk?" I asked.

"A demon," Mary answered. "You can't just fall out of love with a snap of your father's fingers. Or could you? Try it, Father. Or maybe we can look in the Yellow Pages for a deprogramming center that deprograms Jewish girls who fall in love with non-Jewish boys. Or am I the first?"

"You're not pregnant, are you? When is this wedding? Are you going to drop out of college?" he asked.

"Absolutely *not*, Father. And we're not getting married until we graduate."

"Oh, I see," he said.

I stood up. "I think I should leave now," I said. "I didn't mean to get everyone upset."

"Mary's upset, Father's upset, Joseph's upset. Let's all sit quietly for a few minutes and drink our tea," Mary's mother said.

"Joey, don't sit down," Mary's father said.

Mary stood up next to me with her arms crossed and her jaw dropped. Her mother said, "What!" It wasn't a question; it was an act of defiance.

"It's your turn to shoot, Joey," he said, looking at me. He set his cue stick in the free-standing cue rack that was by the couch and headed our way.

I was not thinking straight, which is not unusual for me. But this time I was not thinking straight *at all*. I turned quickly toward the pool, er snooker table, to hide tears. The first one came when I thought that I destroyed her family, if not the entire Jewish race, and then a happy tear after I realized her father was telling me to shoot, in other words not to leave. I thought trying to make a few shots might steady my nerves. I was able to sink seven balls and made it to the end of the rack. I did not have an easy break shot. "My father said I might be part Jewish. He didn't say that exactly. But he said that Italians and Jews have been marrying each other since at least the Roman times. That's why we have the same noses. I'm probably more Jewish than Mary and Doctor Hannah. They have movie star noses. I don't know for sure, but Doctor Malin, you might have Italian blood in you. Don't we have the same nose?" I was standing there rubbing the blue chalk on my cue stick the whole time. My hands were turning blue.

"I'm sure your father meant well," Doctor Malin said. "But what do *your* parents think? Don't they want your kids to be raised Catholic?"

"I don't think they'll care, as long as Mary and I love each other. I told them I wanted to marry Mary, and they didn't say anything about raising our kids Catholic."

"Well, how could you even get married? I know our Rabbi won't perform the wedding. A Catholic priest won't either. Who would marry you?"

"I'm not a practicing Catholic."

Then Mary's mother added, "Mary's not an observant Jew, and neither am I. What's all the fuss?"

Mary had moved to the couch and had Moses on her lap. "Father, my roommate on campus is a Unitarian. She said her minister would marry us."

"Well, there you are, Hannah. You got your wish, a Catholic boy—a *sheigetz*, marrying a Jewish girl, with a wedding by a Unitarian minister. That's mixing the gene pool. Meh!"

"I whispered to Mary, "What's a sheigetz?"

"That's a non-Jewish boy. Shhhhh," she said. "Father, I've never told you or Mother, but as a teenager in high school, I have quietly wondered if I would change from Reform Judaism to Reconstructionist Judaism when I became an adult. And now I sometimes question if in fact I am better suited for Humanistic Judaism than Reconstructionist Judaism. I still believe—strongly in fact—that God exists. But he is El Shaddai, truly God Almighty, in charge of an entire universe, a universe that is ten or twenty billion light-years wide, not a neurotic father-figure who punishes his children for every transgression, micromanaging the lives of humans, humans who in this great universe are but tiny specks of dust. For that matter, our planet is but a tiny speck of dust, and so is our entire solar system. A light year is six trillion miles wide. The universe is ten or twenty *billion* times six *trillion* miles wide. Someone please, just tell me why God Almighty, who created us in his *own* image, as his *chosen* people, had to make the universe so *large*. It seems like an awful waste of space, no pun intended."

"Okay, Mary, Joseph, and Joachim, as a momentous occasion, this is right up there with our *own* marriage and even the birth of Mary. It would not be unwise for everyone to sleep on it before discussing it further. So why don't you finish your game and talk about something nice? How about your classes. Take turns telling about the hardest and easiest classes you had this year, and Joachim tell about the hardest and easiest classes you taught this year. Just anything. Oh, Joey, Mary told us a little about your grandfather's wine making. Why don't you tell Joachim about that? I'm going upstairs to start dinner."

We managed to follow her instructions and even to play another round to a hundred and twenty-five points. Mary won both games. Her father learned more about making wine than he probably wanted to know. And I was pleased to learn that Doctor Malin enjoyed a glass of Chianti when eating at various Italian restaurants, both in North Jersey and in the city. He explained how he managed to keep kosher in Italian restaurants by sticking with seafood dishes like Branzini, Striped Bass or Trout over a bed of linguine, or Pasta Primavera, and his favorite when available, Tagliatelle with Truffles, sprinkled with black pepper and Pecorino-Romano cheese. He would steer clear of the shellfish and the meat dishes, because they were not kosher.

I felt like he was warming up to me a little. When I told him that my father won't eat lamb because his pet lamb was served for dinner, I had to conceal my great joy when he replied that he would have to remind his wife not to make her lamb stew when my parents come for dinner.

Mary's mother called down for us to wash up for dinner. She made a chicken stew, or a very hearty chicken soup, with carrots, celery, onions, matzah balls, and a slight hint of dill.

"Have you eaten matzah balls before, Joey?"

"No, Doctor Hannah, but this reminds me of my mom's chicken and dumplings. It's delicious."

"When your parents came for dinner? He said that?" Mary said when we talked on the phone later that week.

"Yes, he did. I don't think he realized what he said. But I found out that he liked Italian wine. Well, Chianti at least. He thanked me when I told him I would bring some of my grandfather's wine the next time I visit."

The Colocento Family Episode

WE SAW EACH OTHER EVERY OTHER WEEKEND THROUGH
most of the summer. I would go to my parents' or wherever
my family was gathering on the alternate weekends. We
wrote letters on the weekends that we didn't see each other.

Dear Mary,
When we're apart I feel like a starving, bedraggled orphan in
an orphanage. I'm in a cold, damp basement room, just
slightly larger than a closet. The orphanage is run by the
Sisters of Our Lady of Infinite Mercy. You'd think they
would try to live up to their namesake, but all they ever feed
us is lukewarm porridge. It's rather thin too. There's a mouse
in my room, who sleeps under my bed. I was going to name
him Giacobbe, after my father. But he has long whiskers that
make him look like a conquistador, so I named him
Alphonso. I found him a tri-cornered, feathered hat that was
with some dolls in an old toy box that someone donated. The
hat looks like it came off a doll's costume of some sort.
Alphonso's such a character, a personage is more like it. He'll
probably steal the show from me in this letter. After all, I'm

the protagonist here; this is my love letter. He eats most of the porridge, because I can't stand it. I'd have starved to death long ago if it weren't for Alphonso. He has a trick he uses to get the cheese and the peanut butter from the dozens of mouse traps set all over the orphanage that the nuns use to catch mice. He's a cheese snob, and won't eat the stale cheddar that they use for the traps. (I bet he would love some Pecorino-Romano or some creamy Gorgonzola.) So he eats the peanut butter and brings me the stale cheese. Keeps me going. I just hope I can live long enough to catch one more glimpse of your goddess-like visage. Did I hear you say next weekend? Very well then, next weekend. Now I have something to live for. If I start to nibble your ears, please don't take offense. I'm probably just hungry.

I'm plum crazy about you,

Joey

P.S. Alphonso says, "Buenas Tardes."

Dear Joey,

I find my love for you expressed in bits and pieces that I can pick and choose from the Song of Solomon: Let him kiss me with the kisses of his mouth--for thy love is better than wine. Tell me, O thou whom my soul loveth, where thou feedest, where thou makest thy flock to rest at noon. Hark! My beloved! Behold, he cometh, leaping upon the mountains, skipping upon the hills. My beloved is mine, and I am his. Joey, you have lured me into your gravitational field, stronger than the sun's, and I cannot escape.

I Love You,

Mary

(Please permit me one very last itsy bitsy, teeny weeny aside. There will not be any more. I'm certain. By now my readers must surely understand that I would never tell a deliberate lie. I may get my facts mixed up from time to time, but I will never lie to you on purpose. So, you can imagine when I read that particular letter from Mary that I almost had a heart attack. That coffee-stained letter is still in my possession. I don't want to digress, except to explain that I had just taken a gulp of coffee before delving into Mary's letter. I choked on it and coughed coffee out of my mouth, while at the same time it was coming straight out of my nose.)

If we mailed our letters by Wednesday after the weekend that we saw each other, then they usually arrived by the Saturday or Monday of the following weekend. On the first weekend apart after my visit to her house, I didn't receive her letter by Monday, Tuesday, or Wednesday. I imagined that her father's wish came true, that she had just tired of me. But Thursday I received a letter stamped AIRMAIL—the first airmail letter I probably ever received, from a place called Villebon Sur Yvette, in France. She had managed to get a last-minute plane ticket to accompany her mother to Paris for a few days, where her mother was to speak at a conference, and they stayed with a colleague in that little village on the outskirts of Paris.

"Je t'adore et tu me manques tellement," she wrote, and fortunately she translated, "I adore you and miss you so much," which meant that she would still come to meet my parents that coming Saturday. Her mother offered to bring her down to Princeton before noon. Then I would drive her to Bridgeview for an afternoon and dinner with my parents. The hard part would be driving her the hundred miles all the way to Cedar Mills after dinner, then turning around to drive sixty more miles back to Princeton.

"Joey, I love your Mary here. You *need* a Jewish wife.

Jews are smart. My doctor's Jewish, Doctor Greenspan. You should see the sculptures in his waiting room. He sculpts with an Italian clay, *plastilina* he calls it. Then he has them cast in bronze. He's a Jewish Renaissance man. Mary can give you the mental stimulation you need."

"Ma, I keep telling you, the last thing in the world that I need is more mental stimulation. But I am madly in love with this girl, who happens to be much smarter than me."

Then my dad interrupted, "Jews are smart, but so are Italians, that Leonardo de Angelo guy."

"It's da Vinci, Dad, Leonardo da Vinci."

"What do *I* know?" He says this all the time and always throws his hands up when he does. "Okay, da Vinci. He painted the Mona Lisa and the Last Supper. And he invented the first helicopter."

Mom's talking at the same time, so I couldn't say that Dad actually interrupted her. I may have mentioned earlier that Italians all talk in unison. "She's much prettier than you too. I mean she's too pretty for you. I didn't expect you to find a girl so pretty. Red hair? Look at that, a Jewish girl with red hair."

Mom and Dad were both talking at once and Mary's head was swiveling back and forth between them, trying to keep up. She would glance at Mom, blushing from the compliments, then turn to Dad, trying to look as serious as if she were attending a lecture by an esteemed Renaissance scholar.

Mom made a spinach lasagna in a white cream sauce, similar to an Alfredo sauce. With it we had broiled flounder. For dessert my mom made a homemade Italian cheesecake; in our family it was always topped with crushed pineapple and sprinkled with cinnamon. Dinner was a much more joyous affair at my parents' than at Mary's parents', since my mom and dad were both excited about our engagement. My dad was a little disappointed that we were waiting until we graduated. He was anxious to have grandchildren. "Why can't Mary watch the kids while you're in school?"

"Dad, we're *both* in school. And we're probably both going to grad school, Mary first. So we're not going to rush into having kids. We're getting married next June, after we graduate."

"Then she could commute to Rutgers in Camden for grad school. The two of you can live here and your mom can watch the kids. Doesn't Rutgers have a grad school in Camden? I know they have a law school down there. My cousin Bene's kid went there."

"Dad, Mary's going to grad school at Princeton. When people go to grad school they're not just looking at a school, but at a specific professor. Mary has a chance to study with a world renowned philosopher at Princeton. It's that guy I told you about, with the cracked mosaics."

"How do you like the flounder, Mary?"

"Oh, it's delicious, Mrs. Colocento."

"Just call me Rachel, Mary. After you're married, you'll have to call me 'mom.' I always wanted a second child, but couldn't have one. You'll be the daughter I always wanted."

"Let her use the Italian pronunciation," my dad said, sounding it out for her, "In Italian Rachel has an e on the end, so it's Rah-KEL-li, she'll be your Mama Ra-KEL-li."

"She'll be my Mama Ra-KEL-li also, because Mary's mom will be Mama Malin," I said.

"Okay then, Future Mama Ra-KEL-li, the sauce tastes like Chablis. Is that Chablis?" Mary asked.

"No that's a Pinot Grigio," Dad said. "That flounder came from your uncle Albert, Joey. We went down to

Hammonton to see them yesterday. The spinach is from your Aunt Maria's greenhouse."

"Hammonton is more Italian than Italy, Mary," I said. "Uncle Al and Aunt Maria have a small blueberry farm there."

"It's not small," Dad said, "it's twenty acres."

"How are they?" I asked. We're all talking at the same time.

"That is small," Mom said. "Albert said himself that it was small."

"That's because my brother doesn't like to brag. He's not like that."

"They're fine," Mom said. Maria just got over a cold, she caught from Little Al when he came home from the Navy last weekend."

"He's not little anymore," Dad said. "He's bigger than his dad now."

"What's he doing in the Navy?" I said. "Is he at the Philly Navy Yard?"

"No, he's down by Virginia Beach," Mom said.

"He's in Dam Neck, Virginia," Dad said. "He's in electronics in the Polaris missile program."

"He was always smart," Mom said. "Not bookworm smart like you are, Joey—"

"But he rebuilt his dad's diesel tractor engine just by reading about it in a Chilton's manual," Dad said.

"Well, I hope he doesn't go to Vietnam," I said.

"That's done," Mom said. "Vietnam is over."

"I haven't been paying attention," I said.

"He's not good at paying attention," Mary finally got a word in.

"Oh, we know, we know," both parents said in unison.

"You lost a cousin in Vietnam, Joey, your cousin Vito," Dad said.

"I have, I mean I *had* a Cousin Vito? I didn't know I had a Cousin Vito," I said.

"He's your second cousin, Joey. He's my cousin Vito's son; he was in the Army," Dad said.

I was hoping to get on the road by seven o'clock, since we had a long drive to Mary's house, plus my drive back to Princeton. But Mom insisted that I have a cup of coffee to counteract the small glass of Pinot Grigio I had with dinner. So we got out of there around seven-thirty.

I pulled up in her driveway just before nine-thirty. As I opened her door for her, I very clumsily got down on one knee, thinking this was as good a time as any to propose. "Is this a good time to propose?"

She answered with a long kiss that probably lasted only a few seconds or so, but seemed a lot longer. I was scared to death that her parents might be looking out the windows at us. "You already know my answer, sweetie. But I want this 'momentous occasion,' as Mother will surely call it, to be extra special. Mother is bringing me to Princeton on Friday, so I can get some more library books. And I have some other books that are due then. Can you take time off from your work Friday? She could drop me off and you can bring me home later. We could have a picnic at Lake Carnegie. That would be a nice place for it. I'll pack a lunch at home and bring it.

The Sailboat Episode

If you want to find paths, you should also not spurn madness, since it makes up such a great part of your nature.

— C.G. Jung (in *NYT*, 9/20/2009)

.

I HAD ALL WEEK TO PREPARE. MY BRILLIANT IDEA WAS to get permission to use one of the Laser sailboats down at the boathouse. I would propose to Mary while out for a sail on Lake Carnegie. I learned to sail on a friend's Sunfish the summer before my senior year in high school. His parents had a cottage by Mirror Lake in Browns Mills, and I spent a week there learning to sail. It was not enough experience to get me on the Princeton Sailing Team, but I was able to join the Sailing Club.

The Laser is similar to a Sunfish. They're both about fourteen feet long. The laser had a jib sail, but I never learned how to use it. I would just use the mainsail. I had sailed the Laser only a couple of times in my freshman year, before realizing that I would not have much time for sailing at Princeton. I did not have the academic preparation that some of my classmates had, which meant that I would have to spend more time studying.

Doctor Hannah dropped Mary off in the boathouse parking lot as planned. Mary didn't know that we were going for a sail. "Don't worry, Doctor Hannah, I'll have her home before sunset," I said.

"It doesn't matter to me, Joseph, but Joachim will like that. Enjoy your picnic now."

Earlier that day I paddled the boat under the Washington Road bridge before *stepping* the mast, so that we could have a pleasant sail up to the next bridge and back. I had just finished rigging the Laser, and tied it up to a tree on the bank. The retractable daggerboard-keel and the rudder would be put in place after we shoved off. It was a beautiful sunny day in the mid-seventies, with a good breeze, a perfect day for sailing. With the picnic lunch and some of my Nonno's wine carefully stowed in the cockpit storage bin, we donned our life jackets, hoisted the sail and got underway. The wind was behind us, out of the south, so sailing up toward the Harrison Street bridge on a *broad reach* was very pleasant.

As we approached the bridge, I let the sail down as I turned the rudder to ease us under the shade of some trees on the southeast side of the lake. I tied us up to a tree root that was sticking out of the water, and then got straight to the business at hand. It was awkward trying to get down on one knee on such a small boat. The Laser is relatively stable under sail, but very wobbly at a standstill. (No, I did not fall overboard.)

Mary thought it would be a "momentous occasion" if I were to propose while we were having a picnic by Lake Carnegie. I thought it would be "extra momentous" if I did it on this little sailboat. I was also under the impression that I was supposed to say something memorable, for which I racked my brain for the entire week. What *sprung to mind* (I should be very wary of things that spring to mind) was my weird take on something I learned in a biology class. "Mary, I think you already know that I love you madly. I see us as two peas in a pod, a Mendelian pod, two long and slender, slightly twisted RNA-like, half-cells of flesh, mind and spirit, two gametic counterparts—"

"Comedic?"

"No, gametic. An RNA strand is a gamete. But you're right—two gametic-*comedic* counterparts, longing to become interwoven in a DNA-like union of zygotic bliss."

"Psychotic?"

"No, zygotic. DNA formed from the RNA of two parents is a zygote. But I like that, a DNA-like union of zygotic-*psychotic* bliss. This is my way of saying will you marry me?"

"Yes, I'll marry you, Joseph. But that is probably the strangest marriage proposal that has ever been uttered."

"I suspected that, just further evidence that I was a hay-fever admit, as Tiger said."

"Well, Mother will ask how you proposed. I'll tell her that you made it very special, by taking me sailing, and then asking me while we stopped in a quiet little cove for an onboard picnic. And of course I'll tell her how you got down on one knee and said, 'Will you marry me?'"

"I would not tell her all the biological stuff; she might take it wrong."

"That's exactly what I was thinking, sweetheart. See, we *are* two peas in a pod." With that I clumsily put my great-grandmother's engagement ring on her finger. "I'm sorry it's such a small diamond, but it was my great-grandmother's engagement ring. My great-grandfather was a stone mason in Italy."

"It's a lovely ring, Joey."

After a picnic lunch of egg salad sandwiches, Jello with a variety of fruit suspended in it for dessert, and some of Nonno's wine to toast our future life together, I untied the boat and headed us back toward the Washington Road bridge. By now the wind had shifted from southerly to southwesterly, so it was coming straight at us. Going against the wind requires you to sail diagonally, *tacking* or zig-zagging back and forth, on a *close reach*, from one bank to the other. It takes much longer to sail a given distance than sailing with the wind at your back. Our fifteen-minute sail with the wind took almost forty-five minutes heading back against the wind, which had nearly doubled in velocity.

When we got just above the Washington Road bridge I was quite proud that my *close reach* heading to *starboard* would allow me to beach the sailboat by steering it a little more to the right. Now we were perpendicular to the wind, which would have put us on a *broad reach*, had I remembered to let out the sail. Instead, because I had the *sheet*--the rope that controls the sail--looped around a cleat in position for sailing forty-five degrees to the wind, instead of ninety degrees, the boat capsized immediately. We could have done without the life jackets; the water was only about four feet deep, but wet suits would have been nice. While the temperature that day was in the mid to upper seventies, the water was still quite cold in late June.

The first thing we had to do, I told Mary, was don't panic, because the boat was easy to turn upright. We just had to get around to the daggerboard-keel and put our weight on it, to give us enough leverage to right the boat. Mary was wearing tennis sneakers, but I was wearing those sandals I hated. As soon as I took a step, one sandal and then the other came off my feet in the soft mud. I retrieved them, but there was no point in wearing them yet. Mary walked around to the keel, while I doggy paddled to it, because the mud in my toes felt very creepy.

We tried putting our weight on the daggerboard, but the boat wouldn't budge. "It looks like the sail is full of water," Mary said.

"Oh, that's funny. These things are supposed to right themselves pretty easily this way. Oops, wait a minute," I said as I started to paddle back around the boat. "I forgot to release the sail sheet from the cleat. That's why it's full of water." After releasing the sheet and paddling back around the boat to the daggerboard, we were able to right it. I won't say it was easy, because we both weighed so little that we had to try a few different ways to concentrate our weight on the very outermost tip of the daggerboard. We finally did it with Mary sitting on my shoulders, while I leaned both elbows on the tip. It righted itself so fast that my elbows slipped off it, and with Mary on my shoulders, I ended up slapping my face into the water to get a mouthful and nose full of lake water.

When we got the boat back to shore, Mary went to get her windbreaker out of the car for herself and my old wool sweater out of the trunk for me, while I started taking down the mast so I could row the boat back under the bridge. If I can be forgiven for one small aside, it's no small task to pull a wool sweater over a wet torso.

After we got the boat dragged back up on shore to the place where I found it that morning, and the sails stowed in the boathouse locker, we went straight to my Spelman dorm, where we both changed into some of my dry clothes, after which I took our wet clothes to the laundry room. "We're in luck," I said. "I didn't have to wait for a washer."

"That's good, I was wondering how to explain to Father why my clothes smelled like tadpoles."

"They're plentiful this time of year; I should have checked our pockets."

The Neutral Beach Episode

"... because even if Ales has been dead a long time she's still there in the house, I think, and I think that I should have found myself a dog because I've always liked dogs, and cats too, but I'd rather have a dog, there can be a greater friendship with a dog, I think and I've thought it so many times but I've never gone ahead and done it, got a dog, I don't really know why, maybe it's because I'd still rather be alone with Ales? Because even though she's dead she's still there in a way..."

— Jon Fosse (*The Other Name: Septology*)

It was Saturday, May 20th, 1978. Mary, Tiger and I had all completed our senior theses and taken all of our final exams. Tiger's skinny hi-rise earned him an A-plus. Mary's thesis earned her an A, and I got a C. It could have been the crazy C that I mentioned earlier. I'm not sure. Jaynes and Kaufmann both shot down my idea to see if mescaline helps you to better understand Nietzsche. But I convinced Professor Jaynes to let me conduct an experiment to see if LSD expanded consciousness. I had three volunteer subjects, my Alice Cooper concert friends from Camden. I would ask them questions based on Timothy Leary's "reality tunnels" and Peter Wason's "confirmation bias," before and during an LSD trip. They were all gainfully employed, but they "tripped" most weekends, on Saturday nights. I thought I had good results, and so did Professor Jaynes, who gave me a B. But senior theses get graded by another professor besides your advisor. It was my "good fortune" to get Charlie Gross, a renowned neuroscientist who studied the visual cortex of monkey brains, as my second reader. He said that my thesis was more an anecdote than an experiment, and besides that, my sample size was too small, which would have put me in the C category. But because in his view my writing made him believe that I was actually on LSD when I wrote it, he gave me a D, which they averaged with the B for a passing grade of C. It was time to celebrate.

We decided to grab some hoagies from Hoagie Haven, then drive down to Barnegat Lighthouse State Park and climb to the top of the lighthouse. We had talked about going there since the previous summer. On the map it looked about halfway between the North Jersey and South Jersey shore areas that our two families visited—a neutral beach, we thought. We took the back roads and got there around noon. It was a sunny day and the temperature was supposed to climb into the eighties. We were prepared for it to be much cooler. That time of year especially, the shore can be ten or twenty degrees colder than inland, depending on the wind direction. The wind was coming from the west, so it was quite warm. Mary wore a one-piece yellow swimsuit under denim cutoffs with a grey Princeton sweatshirt. I was dressed for the weather to go in either direction, with gym shorts under khakis, and a long-sleeved paisley shirt over a tee shirt. I remember the paisley shirt, because it was a Christmas present when I was sixteen and it still fit. My mom had sewn denim patches on the elbows when I wore them out. All of Tiger's clothes pretty much came from Brooks Brothers, LL Bean, or Princeton's U-store. Today he had on bright red, dressy looking shorts—the kind that I imagined men wore on a golf course, and a white sweatshirt from which he cut off the sleeves.

Tiger rode in the front and Mary stretched out, in a manner of speaking, on the VW's back seat. When we got there the lighthouse was closed for repairs, so we decided to take a walk along the beach instead. First we spread our army blanket and some towels on the sand to eat our hoagies. There were just a few other people along the beach. The following weekend this place would be packed with Memorial Day vacationers, celebrating the beginning of the summer season at the shore.

"Tiger, why don't you walk with us?" I said.

"Yes, Tiger, that would be great," Mary said.

"Why don't you two run with me? I'm going to run about ten miles," Tiger said.

Mary spoke for us both, "We're not runners. You better take it easy, Tiger. You can overheat in this weather."

"Yes, Tiger. Don't overdo it."

"I run ten miles or more several times a week," he said. "I was prepared to run up and down the lighthouse stairs a few times. That would have been more strenuous than my usual ten-mile run. It's the kind of stamina I need for sparring in tournaments." With that he took off down the beach.

Tiger said that he made it to Surf City, about seven miles away, where he bought a soda and then ran back. In the meantime, Mary and I walked as far as the town of Harvey Cedars, a few miles away, before turning back. She had ditched her sweatshirt when we parked the car, and was wearing my long-sleeved shirt and my slightly-rolled-up khakis, along with a wide brimmed straw hat, to keep from getting sunburned. On our walk back we stopped every so often to cool off in the water, just ankle to knee deep, but it felt very refreshing. The water was still ice cold. Tiger passed us on his way back.

We sat on the blanket for a while, watching the seagulls' antics and several sandpipers scurrying about. Tiger was sitting at the water's edge, with his legs stretched out in front of him, getting drenched by the waves, along with a sea foam bath.

"I love the sound of seagulls," Mary said. "I have so many pleasant memories of going to Point Pleasant with my parents and hearing the seagulls since as early as I can remember."

"Me too. Every summer my aunt Isabelle rented a big house in Margate for a week, and the whole family would stay there for at least a few days. We would all walk down to the beach by Lucy the elephant."

"Lucy the elephant? What's that?"

"You never heard of Lucy? It's this big old elephant five or six stories tall that's right on the beach in Margate. We always use it as a landmark to find each other at the beach. Some days there's twenty or thirty family members meeting up on the beach. You can't miss Lucy, so that's where we'd meet."

"What's it made out of? What is it used for?"

"I think it's wood, and maybe tin siding. It's not being used for anything; it's all run down. Except my cousin Nick said it's getting restored now."

"That's so neat, Joe. Will you take me to see it sometime?"

"Sure, sweetheart, I'll take you this summer to our next family gathering there. Everyone will be at our wedding, except Lucy of course."

"Just think, Joey, in three weeks we'll be married. I'll be Mrs. Joseph Colocento, otherwise known as Mrs. Joey Nostrils."

"In a few years you'll be Dr. Mary Colocento. You can't say Dr. Joseph Colocento or Dr. Joey Nostrils."

"I know, silly, but to my close friends, I'll go by Mrs. Joey Nostrils."

"Well, I still have to pinch myself. You still want to marry me? You're like a model. You're like Twiggy with red hair. I take that back; you're even prettier than Twiggy."

"Thank you, sweetie. But I do still want to marry you, more each day." Then she pointed at two seagulls flying in a tight circle overhead. Do you remember hearing that since childhood?"

"My aunts would save stale bread and let us feed the seagulls. They just asked us to keep away from everyone else when we did it, so the seagulls didn't drop bird doo on somebody's head. We would throw pieces of the bread up in the air and they would catch it in midflight. My cousin Nick would hold his arm up with a piece of bread and a seagull would take it out of his hand."

"Joey, honey, you say you don't sunburn, but your legs are beet red. We'd better get out of the sun now. Let's head back to campus. It's already five o'clock."

"Tiger, come on, we're going to leave now," I said.

"I'm ready. I'll use that outdoor shower to rinse off the salt water. I don't want shotgun. I'll take a nap in the back while you and Mary get us home."

"There's not much room to stretch out back there," Mary said. "I'll put my seat as far forward as it will go. Then you can lean against the window behind Joey and put your feet down on the floor behind me."

"That sounds great, Mary. I think the sun tired me out more than running."

We took the same pleasant back roads home that we used that morning. I remember Mary getting a small tube of lotion from her purse. Tiger was asleep in the backseat and snoring loudly. I was squinting from the sun coming in the windshield, and reached up to turn down the visor, just as Mary leaned over to rub lotion on my knee and lower thigh. My VW was not air conditioned. The lotion felt warm from being in Mary's purse all day. Feeling Mary's warm hand rubbing warm lotion on my leg made me instinctively look over at her and sigh with delight. She looked into my eyes and smiled—the most beautiful smile.

That's the last thing I remember. I don't remember going through a stop sign. I don't remember my jaw shattering as it hit the steering wheel, or being thrown out of the car door the instant before it went under the flatbed truck. The accident report said it was carrying milk, quart and half gallon glass bottles, in plastic cases, on wooden pallets. I don't remember landing on my back on the pavement and chipping three vertebrae. The doctors said they would heal in place. But they wired my jaw shut, which would stay that way for six weeks. I woke up after the anesthesia wore off, and had to be told what happened. When they removed the wires, I was left with an underbite that was not there before. They said it was the closest they could get it, because my jaw was fractured in several places.

Tiger's head slammed into the back of my seat. He had a cracked skull and suffered brain damage to his left temporal lobe, which is generally associated with language abilities. He was in a coma that lasted for five days. When he awoke from it the doctors said they weren't sure if he was able to understand what happened to him. After forty-five years, I'm still not sure if he understands.

The doctors told me Mary died from severe head trauma, which I still cannot think about without having an emotional meltdown. They thought it might comfort me to know that she probably died before she knew what hit her. God blocks it from our memory, or does nature? Is nature compassionate? Why would nature have compassion? Maybe that's one argument for the existence of God that makes sense. To this day I can't remember a thing about the accident that happened after turning and seeing Mary's piercing gaze into my eyes.

What was she thinking when she looked into my eyes just before the crash? She was fond of the Song of Solomon. I pore through its verses to this day, wondering what she was thinking. Was it this verse? No, that's not it. Was it that one? Not likely. How about this one? Well, it's certainly prophetic, "His eyes are as the eyes of doves by the rivers of waters, washed with *milk*, and fitly set." I had nightmares for years about milk from broken bottles pouring down on her head and mixing with her blood. The sight or even the thought of strawberry milkshakes makes me gasp with horror.

My ranting and raving at God for years afterwards, generally took the form of, "If I find out that Mary experienced any pain, if you didn't shut her conscious down, before impact, then I will make Nietzsche's statement come true, that God is dead, because I will come up there—wherever you are hiding, and kill you myself, with my bare hands. You hear me, you? And then every curse word in the English language, plus a few that I knew in Italian, as well as some that I made up on the spot. This went on for over three decades, until our kitchen encounter ten years ago. Of course I asked him.

He said, "I took her before the crash."

"That's what I *said*. You *took* her."

"Joseph. Joseph. Joseph, when are you going to face it, that the accident took her *life*; I took her *soul*. I know you still blame yourself. That's why you're so mad at *me*. You couldn't stand to be that angry at *yourself*. You didn't kill her. Do I have to explain that an accident is what it's called when something bad happens that no one intended?"

"But wait. Didn't you just say that you took her *before* the crash? Did *you* kill her?"

"Oh, Joseph. Nature sometimes, but not always, blocks severe trauma from the memory, as it did with your memory of the crash. But when anyone is about to die, from an accident, from ill health, or any other cause, the soul leaves the body a few minutes earlier. The moment you turned to look at her, she was gone. Let's just say that she came home. I can tell you that she's happy now, but that she loved you dearly. That's the most I can say. I can tell you that your soul will vividly remember your very last life on earth. The happy memories will stay with you for an eternity, and the bad memories will quickly fade. Fatal trauma is erased permanently the moment before it occurs. I took care of that before you were created."

Her parents wouldn't talk to me at the funeral. Her father gave me a very angry look as he walked away. Her mother put her finger to her mouth as I approached her, signaling that she didn't *want* to hear, or wasn't *ready* to hear anything I had to say. She started bawling and turned away. It was only after about five years of running into each other at Mary's grave, both sniveling from a good cry, that she approached me, gave me a warm hug, and said, "It was an accident, Joey. I don't blame you, or him anymore," she pointed up in the sky. "And please don't blame yourself."

I wasn't blaming myself then. It was only after my encounter with God that, slowly, over a period of years, I stopped blaming him, and replaced it with blaming myself. I killed her, just as surely as if I were Hendrix's "Hey Joe" and shot her. I took my eyes off the road for more than a split second, and a split second is all it takes. I should have known better.

Epilogue – Chaos Theory and the Nature of God

In the beginning there was an explosion. At about one-hundredth of a second, the temperature of the universe was about a hundred thousand times a million degrees Centigrade. As the explosion continued the temperature dropped. Much later, after a few hundred thousand years, it would become cool enough for electrons to join with nuclei to form atoms of hydrogen and helium, The resulting gas would begin, under the influence of gravitation, to form clumps, which would ultimately condense to form the galaxies and stars of the present universe.

— Steven Weinberg (*The First Three Minutes*)

I SHOULD SAY AT LEAST A WORD OR TWO ABOUT MARY'S thesis, because it turns out that the quantum mechanics of the soul are intertwined with Mary's conclusions about the nature of God.

She did not resort to fractal geometry or other

sophisticated mathematics that chaos theory would use to study complexity in the material world. Instead, to uncover the nature of God, a question at the heart of the metaphysical world, she resorted to a process similar to my Nonna making Cioppino Stew. First she gathered all the information she could and sifted it down to short notes—the *ingredienti primi,* like Nonna's raw ingredients—on color coded index cards (post it notes weren't invented yet), which she taped all over the walls by her bed in her dorm room. Then she let it swirl around in her subconscious, like Nonna stirred the stew. Her hope was that the chaotic mixture, to which she kept adding ingredients, would reach its bifurcation point, like in the Belousov-Zhabotinskii reaction, and organize itself on a higher level, at least before her thesis was due at the end of the school year.

If I may be permitted to digress for one last time, it is worth mentioning two opposing yet relevant sayings. One is that the devil is in the details and the other is that God is in the details. Mary hoped that the latter was true, that God was hidden, but would yet somehow emerge from the subconscious stew. Her details included everything from the primitive concepts of the Sky God and the Great Mother, through Anaximander's *Apeiron* (the infinite), Aristotle's *Unmoved Mover* and *First Cause* (later elaborated by Aquinas), Plotinus's *Henosis,* Anselm's *Ontological Argument,* Spinoza's *Pantheism,* William James's *Varieties of Religious Experience,* Charles Williams's *Co-inherence,* as well as the concepts of God in all of the major religions—Buddhism, Hinduism, Judaism, Christianity, and Islam, including all of their sectarian and mystical variations, not to mention all of the modern philosophical and psychological arguments for and against the existence of God, from Spinoza, Einstein, Russell,

Freud, Hegel, Jung, Nietzsche, Lewis, and many others. And then she juxtaposed all of that with the observations of science and cosmology about the universe.

To summarize her thesis, the universe most likely did not have an anthropomorphic God behind a curtain, like Oz. God may have been the so-called *singularity* that existed before the Big Bang. Physicists say that before the Big Bang, the entire universe was the size of a peach, with a temperature of a quadrillion degrees. Described by physicists as a *plasma*, it was too hot and too dense for protons, neutrons, electrons and all the other subatomic particles to be formed. It was held together by a force that's far more powerful than gravity, far more powerful than electromagnetic forces, and far more powerful than the strong and weak nuclear forces that hold atomic nuclei together. In Mary's words, a *divine plasma* that, perhaps in a moment of exuberance, created the universe as we know it with a Big Bang.

Mary chose to call the force that held it together, prior to the Big Bang, divine attraction. She mentioned Nietzsche's "don't become attached to everything you hatched," only to contradict it with divine attraction. Every particle in the entire expansive universe, which physicists thought was ten or twenty billion light years wide in 1977 (now they think it's ninety-three billion), times 6 trillion miles per light year (give or take), and counting, comes from this point, this *singularity*. Everything, absolutely *everything*, arose from it. So it's no wonder that, like Mark Twain, it might have a preternatural fondness that only a father could feel for everything in the universe. In the same way and for a similar reason that Carl Sagan said we are *stardust*, Mary posited that we are *God-dust* as well, shedding new light on Genesis 3:19, "For dust you are, and to dust you will return."

People come back from near-death experiences describing an intense, bright light; Ezekiel (1:27) describes God as glowing metal, full of fire and surrounded by brilliant light. That sounds like the singularity before the Big Bang. Arguably, there is no need to call it God, to invoke some numinous or divine principle to explain the attraction between the pre-explosion particles. But if you do, then sayings like God is in everything, everything is God, or in Buddhism, everything is *One,* make sense. The practitioners of Christian (Meister Eckhart, etc.), Jewish (Hasidism), Islamic (Sufis, Rumi), Buddhist and Tibetan *mysticism* all converge on a similar concept of the divine, and that our inmost self is wedded to it, or is one and the same as it, or in Mary's view, *entangled* with it.

But does that equate to saying that God is matter, energy, dark matter, dark energy, or all of the above? Or does God both transcend and preexist the Big Bang and the universe? So why even posit a God? Why do western religions say God is a *he,* an omniscient, omnipotent, benevolent, grandfatherly *he?* And why would we say that God loves us? Isn't love a human emotion that we project onto God? Is a God that transcends the universe conscious in the sense that we understand consciousness? Mary was fond of a relatively unknown theologian, Frederic Spiegelberg, who wrote *The Religion of No-Religion,* which was not about atheism, but about a God who was too big to fit in any one box.

And no churches which clasp Him tight
As though a fugitive, then wail over Him
As over a captive and wounded deer.

— Rainer Maria Rilke

Mary chose to refer to God as The Divine, a term that helps to overcome some of our anthropomorphic projections. Mary thought that cosmology and quantum physics did not prove or disprove God's existence, but that they left lots of *room* for The Divine. She suggested that we (and all of matter) are *entangled* with The Divine (as I noted earlier, from *quantum entanglement,* Einstein's "spooky action at a distance"). She did not elaborate on how that might work, except to say that the presence of The Divine in the universe might be mediated through *dark matter,* which she thought was a misnomer. It should be called *hidden matter,* because she thought that it might be the actual presence of The Divine permeating the universe. Matter makes up five percent of the universe. Dark matter accounts for twenty-five percent, and dark energy accounts for seventy percent. The latter two are not *dark,* per se. Because they *can't be seen,* physicists gave them that unfortunate description. Mary wasn't aware of dark energy. It wasn't discovered until the nineteen nineties. If it had been discovered earlier, she would have included it in her thesis as *divine* energy.

She would not have read Dean Radin's 2006 book, *Entangled Minds,* that posits a macro version of quantum entanglement as the process underlying telepathy, and by extension many of the other preternatural ways that we are interconnected, with each other and perhaps with The

Divine. In a recent interview, another contemporary philosopher/computer scientist, Bernardo Kastrup, saw our individual minds as manifestations of one Mind At Large. He used various terms, including *localizations*, *dissociations*, and *doings*. He explained this last term with an analogy of a whirlpool in a river. It seems to have a boundary in the same way our individual minds do, but it is just the river water, water *doing* something—making a whirlpool. Similarly, our minds are all part of one Mind At Large.

> *We see the world piece by piece, as the sun, the moon, the animal, the tree; but the whole, of which these are the shining parts, is the soul.*
>
> — Ralph Waldo Emerson

Also recently, Jeffrey Kripal's 2019 book, *The Flip*, provides a scholarly look at "superhuman" *psi* phenomena that have been extensively documented. Luminaries he mentioned who had direct experience of these phenomena included the philosopher Emanuel Swedenborg, author Mark Twain, physicist Wolfgang Pauli, Nobel Laureate Kary Mullis, philosopher A.J. Ayer, neurosurgeon Eben Alexander, biologist Barbara Ehrenreich, and even the noted sceptic Michael Shermer, among many others. About those "professional intellectuals," Kripal says, "We would do well, though, to listen to these voices, even and especially when they struggle (and finally fail) to make sense of what happened to them." That's an important point. If I were able to make sense of a non-verbal, non-linear encounter with God (or *The Divine*), then it probably wasn't an actual encounter. This may help the publisher's legal department understand why God chose a non-linear-thinking crazy person as the perfect tour guide to the soul.

Physicists, neuroscientists and other *professional* intellectuals create entire philosophies around these experiences because they think that's their job. But their conclusions are just as far-fetched as when some scientists' calculations *proved* that bumblebees can't fly. The calculations merely proved that bumblebees can't *glide*. Like Nietzsche said, systems of thought are often flawed. In the cognitive realm, I imagine that similar miscalculations could prove that the human brain cannot think.

These later insights, discoveries and theories about cosmology, quantum physics, and even metaphysics would have only strengthened Mary's idea that we are made of God-dust. When I told her about them on my most recent visit, she seemed very pleased. She said that Kastrup's whirlpool analogy reminded her of my kitchen encounter, when God said that after death our soul returns to him like a drop of water returning to the sea. At least I think that's what she said; it may have just popped into my head while sitting at her grave.

When all is said and done, the great mereological conundrum arises again: is the whole of the universe greater than the sum of its parts, and a corollary, is our mind greater than the sum of *its* parts? Does the observable brain only account for five percent of the mind, with dark (divine) matter accounting for another twenty-five percent, and dark (divine) energy seventy percent?

Does the sum total of all existence give rise to or derive from something that can be construed as divine? In modern terms, that Mary couldn't foresee, are our minds and souls just millions of independent personal computers, or are we all somehow in a network with a divine central server, the so

Joseph G Mazzilli

called *anima mundi* or *world soul*? And do we externalize
the divinity within (Psalm 82:6 and John 10:34), just like
Jaynes' *The Origin of Consciousness and the Breakdown of
the Bicameral Mind* explains how we externalized our
subconscious in our early history? And lastly, are we like my
friend Adam at the Alice Cooper concert, thinking that
God, who oversees a *ninety-three* billion light-year wide
universe (with as many as a *hundred million* planets with
life forms as technologically advanced as ours, according to
the *Drake Equation*), as well as everything beyond it—
multiverses, parallel universes and so on—to infinity, has
singled us earthlings out for salvation, not all of us, mind
you, just a small portion? If the universe were the size of our
planet, then the earth might be about the size of one
hydrogen atom. Isn't that the height of hubris, perhaps
madness, as noted in my disclaimer?

Afterword

You could say that the deepest religious experiences have to be kept secret and by nature remain secret, and it would be most destructive to tell them to anyone else. The person who knows more than the others is, by that very fact, unendurable for society and a black sheep—that is quite natural.

— Marie-Louise von Franz

I wasn't going to say anything about this. I did not issue God an ultimatum or anything like that. But I did ask. I said, "I don't expect you to do this, based on your horrible track record so far. But I thought it wouldn't hurt to at least ask, and I'm not asking for anything for myself. I'll just spit it out. If I finish this book for you, will you please, just please —this is not an ultimatum, I'm just asking—please, will you give Tiger his speech back?" And I would not be lying if I said I got teary-eyed asking him.

In spite of all the digging in my research on the meaning of life, and of all that Mary's thesis said about the true nature of God, I still talk to him as though he's the petty, control-freak, codependent grandfather-figure, subject to fits of rage, that the authors of the Judeo-Christian scriptures describe, projecting their own codependency onto God.

I know that I have not shared enough about the quantum mechanics of the soul, nor about my encounter with God, that the readers who stayed with me this far deserve. The main reason is that some of the important information that I needed to tell you came to mind at times and in places where I couldn't write it down, and then by the time I got to where I could write it down, it popped out of my head just as quickly as it popped into my head. I remember one incident in particular. I was in the grocery store checkout line when something so important popped into my head that, after explaining my emergency, I asked the cashier for a pen and something to write on. She handed me a pen and a small paper bag, but the pen was out of ink. I hurriedly paid the bill and rushed out to the car, where I kept a small handful of pens in the ashtray. But then whatever it was that popped into my head was gone. That's why I said at the beginning that if I happen to see you reading it, I might have to grab it from your hands and edit it on the spot, and possibly add a footnote or two for information that was lost while in the checkout line, or while in the shower, or while driving over a bridge.

The other reason is alluded to in the von Franz quote above. I don't think that I should share this; jc and I had a big argument about it. It's the most ridiculous thing I ever heard. And I'm not sure if it actually came from the kitchen encounter with God, or if jc is just making it up out of whole cloth. But he says that God said (so it's second-hand information right there) that Jesus was born with a genetic brain anomaly called *unicephalism*. That's jc's word for it, but the medical field has their own name, *holoprosencephaly*, abbreviated as HPE. Jesus did not have a corpus callosum. His left and right brain were one. So whether God or jc put this idea in my head, it must have been swirling around in there when I had the dream about Tiger's carbon fiber skyscraper bending over like a fishing pole and my Nonno having to sew Mary's brain back together.

HPE affects a very small percentage of fetuses, most of which do not survive and are miscarried. Of the very few individuals who survive, just a very small percentage of those make it to adulthood. The condition is usually, but not always, associated with facial abnormalities that lead the doctors to seek tests that reveal the underlying HPE. There is great variety in the severity and types of symptoms. Ten or more specific genes have been linked to HPE, as well as varied chromosomal abnormalities. A related brain anomaly is *Agenesis of the Corpus Callosum*, or ACC, where the brain is missing the corpus callosum, resulting in a *split brain*.

Is it possible that Jesus's unique genetic variation of HPE made him divine, that it had a critical mass of *divinity* —for lack of a better word—that enabled him to walk on water, turn water into wine, heal the sick and so on? Consider Kim Peek, the mega-savant who inspired the movie *Rain Man*. His unique genetic variation of ACC made him one of the most, if not *the* most prodigious savant in recorded history. His abilities were far broader than portrayed in the movie, perhaps aided by his macrocephaly, an enlarged head and brain. He memorized about ten thousand books in his lifetime, in addition to the more common savant abilities, such as memorizing phone books, maps, zip codes, and calendar calculations. Most savants do not have all of these abilities in combination. Kim's unique ability was not only that he could memorize so many books, but that he read two pages of a book at the same time, one with each eye, and that he read a whole page in about ten seconds. Then he would retain about ninety-eight percent of what he read for the rest of his life, in addition to having all of the more common savant abilities in combination.

Scientists theorize that the brain has far more capacity than we can use. It's commonly thought that the left brain's thought processes are linear, and the right brain's are non-linear. On one level that may be true. But that dichotomy more aptly describes, respectively, the conscious and subconscious. Anything arising from the subconscious is subjected to forced linearity at the conscious level. It's like driving a seven-hundred-plus-horsepower Ferrari with a governor on it that won't let you drive over thirty-five miles per hour. Scientists estimate that the brain could store a petabyte of information. That's equivalent to a computer that could store a quadrillion bytes, in other words a billion megabytes, equivalent to all the information on the entire internet—all the articles, letters, books, music, videos, graphics, social media, emails, etc.

Obviously we don't use this much of our brain, and we most likely don't have access to most of it, except in cases of genetic anomalies or brain injuries. As astonishing as Kim Peek's memory feats are, he still hadn't scratched the surface of the brain's capacity. We get glimpses of it, through a glass darkly, so to speak, in our dreams. My upbringing included occasional refrains from my father that he might need to "knock some sense into me." That's how most genetic mutations and brain injuries work; it's like getting hit in the head with a hammer. Most of the time you end up dead, or in a coma, or like a vegetable. Only in extremely rare instances does it make you a savant. One of those rare instances is Jason Padgett, who in his early thirties was hit in the head and knocked unconscious in a fight at a bar. He awoke from it as a math genius.

Maybe in another million years or more we will slowly evolve to a time when solving great mathematical conundrums, bending spoons, seeing each other's auras, levitating, making planes disappear, healing the sick and raising the dead will be child's play. Advances in bioengineering and genetic engineering may give us a head start. Other examples of extraordinary, but mostly untapped *superhuman* (to use Kripal's term) mental abilities would include scholarly research at UC Irvine and elsewhere on Hyperthymesia—also known as superior autobiographical memory, the very rare ability of some people (estimated at no more than 100 in the entire world) to remember most facts about most days of their lives, going back to various starting points in their childhood, in addition to scholarly research at UVA and elsewhere on past-life memories in children. Maybe we do come back, in this or other universes. Or, as I learned in my kitchen encounter with God, maybe this is our final reincarnation, and it's our choice to work together to make it a heaven or hell.

Some cosmologists speculate that we do indeed live in a *multiverse*, like God said in my encounter, that there are other universes out there. And some think that there are an *infinite* number of universes, as well as an infinite number of versions of each of us. Mathematicians say that infinity is so large that if you add it to itself, it doesn't equal two times infinity, it just equals itself. If you multiply it times itself, you don't get infinity squared, you just get infinity. They say that no matter how high a number you can imagine, for example a trillion times a trillion times a trillion, a trillion times over, that you are still much closer to zero than you are to infinity. So if I am living out my finite lifetime, but in an infinite number of universes, than it's for as much time as if I lived only one life, but infinitely long—an eternity.

I said earlier that God is too big to put in a box, too big for any one religion to contain. With advances in our understanding of cosmology, we should see that God is too big for any one universe as well. We should see that a God in charge of an infinite number of universes is infinite as well, or at least transcends them in some way. (Perish the thought that there could be separate—

lesser—gods in charge of each individual universe.)

In this universe I fidget and cannot sit still, but in another universe a different version of myself is a great Zen master, who can sit and meditate under the Bodhi tree for weeks at a time without eating. In this universe I am a lowly carpenter living in a two-bedroom bungalow in Saint Augustine, but in another I am a hedge fund manager with a penthouse in Manhattan and a vineyard in Tuscany. In yet another universe I am a starving and thirsty refugee in the Sudan. So there's heaven for you: In one universe you're the *haves*, and in another the *have nots* (one reason why the haves might want to take better care of the have nots). In one universe you're so brilliant it borders on madness, and in another you're so mad it borders on brilliance, or so mentally handicapped that you can't tie your own shoelaces. And at the extremes, in one universe you're Judas, and in another you're the Messiah.

Many philosophers and psychologists believe that we project our own inner qualities onto God, that we externalize, in Feuerbach's words, "the infinity of our own nature." Feuerbach was a materialist, but the mystical strain in all religious traditions leads to a belief that there is something divine at our very core. Deep within us there may be a divine candle that burns so brightly, but it's only rarely, nay extremely rarely on this planet that someone gains access to it. Psalm 82 tells us, *"Ye are Gods, and all of you are children of the most high."* Mary's thesis makes clear that if there is a God, then it's more than possible that some spark of The Divine is encoded in our genes, or at least in our soul—through quantum entanglement, dark matter, dark energy, some other mechanism, or a combination of them—if indeed the mind is more than the sum of its parts.

Postscript

Hence, perhaps, someday the converse of <u>Et Verbum caro factum est</u> will become the epitome of a new Gospel, which will proclaim that the Flesh shall be made the Word and become the Utterance of God.

— Honoré de Balzac (Louis Lampert)

As I finished writing those last few words, "if indeed the mind is more than the sum of its parts," Tiger walks out from his bedroom, takes a look at the piles of typing paper scattered all over the dining room table (my biggest fear besides flying is using a computer, so I type), and says, "What the hell are you writing, Joey?"

Then he proofread my entire first draft in two and a half hours, not as fast as Kim Peek, but respectable for a brain injury savant. (Fortunately for the publisher, Tiger was able to fix dozens of typos.) "Joey, your surname comes from the Latin word for pumpkin," he said. "Maybe your God made you a pumpkin head. Then he cut out eyes to see and ears to hear, and he put a candle in your hollow center to shine out.

Postscript

Personally, I think you westerners invented a God because you can't let go of your imaginary friends from childhood. Where's my wooden dummy? Did you get rid of my wooden dummy? And, Joey, you must admit that this book proves what I've been saying all along, that you were a hay fever admit to Princeton."

Prepublication Reviews

I felt like I was being threatened with a chain saw throughout the entire novel. At the same time I understood that he was just kidding.

— Ba'al Shem Tov

While he has increased mankind's understanding of me a trillion-fold, this writer still hasn't the foggiest idea who I am. I am infinite.

— Ein Sof

One has to allow a little more time than usual for a madman to gather his thoughts. That being said, I felt like I was being hacked to shreds with a machete throughout the entire novel.

— God

Prepublication Reviews

There are no words. Even if there were words, I would keep silent.

— Buddha

Glossary

(Most of these words just popped into my head while writing. I had no idea what they meant.)

Analects – sayings of Confucius
Bucolic – pleasant, tranquil landscape or countryside
Bumptious – noisily self-assertive, unpleasantly confident
Chthonic – the underworld, dwelling beneath the earth
Coda – the concluding passage or section of a musical composition
Colloquy – a high-level serious conversation
Conjugation – the forms, tenses, gender, number, etc. of verbs
Diaphanous – thinly veiled, translucent, transparent
Declension – the forms, tenses, gender, number, etc. of nouns, pronouns and adjectives
Deliquious - from deliquium, a failure of the mind or mental faculties
Desultory – disconnected, jumping around
Epigenesis – process of development in the womb or in the egg

Glossary

Eructation - belching

Expatiation – an extended discussion or a speech

Expostulation – earnest and kindly protest

Etymology – study of the origin and history of words

Flibberty-gibberty – mental wandering, frivolous, senseless

Gamete – in conception a cell containing RNA from one parent (see *zygote* below)

Gestational – the time in the womb from conception until birth

Hebetude – dullness or lethargy

Ineffable – incapable of being expressed in words

Interdiction – stopping, prohibiting, or forbidding something, for example by legal force

Lucubration – laborious or intensive study

Mereology – concerning the relationship between the parts and the whole

Mimesis – noun: likeness; compare with verb: to mimic

Morphological – concerning the structure of organisms

Muliebrious – feminine beauty, softness

Non Sequitur – saying something that doesn't follow from what was said before

Oeuvre – a work of art, music or literature, or the artist's entire body of work

Olfactory – relating to the sense of smell

Omniscient – all-knowing, someone who knows everything there is to know

Paleontology – study of earth's early history—fossils, dinosaurs, etc.

Pandemonium – noisy confusion, chaos

Permutation – arrangement or rearrangement of the order of objects in a set

Phylogenetic – the origin, history and evolutionary relationships between organisms

Philology – study of language

Pilloried, past tense of pillory – severe public ridicule and humiliation

Propinquity – nearness, proximity

Prosopopoeia – an imaginary, absent or deceased person represented as speaking (usually on a stage)

Quantum Entanglement – when two particles communicate in ways that are indiscernible, faster than the speed of light, no matter how far apart

Remonstration – objection or disapproval

Senescent – growing old, elderly

Serendipitous – lucky coincidence

Sobriquet - nickname

Somnolently - sleepily

Superfetation – superabundant, like gladiolus, hollyhock, or foxglove blooms

Transmogrify – change into something preposterous, a frog into a prince, or a girl into Ben Franklin

Zygote – in conception the first cell with DNA that combines RNA of both parents